CL♣VERLEAF

CALEB PIRTLE III

McLennan HOUSE
WAXAHACHIE

Published by
McLennan House, Inc.
206 South Rogers
Waxahachie, Texas 75165

Library of Congress
Cataloging-in-Publication Data

Pirtle III, Caleb, 1941 -

CLOVERLEAF

1. Title.

ISBN 0-918865-03-4
Library of Congress Catalog Number: 86-50842

Manufactured in the United States of America

First Printing

To Pat and Joy Patterson who know all about the good times and hard times of hauling a horse to a barrel racing event; to their daughter, Carol, who seldom lost; and to her horse, Rebel, who refused to lose.

Acknowledgments

To Janet and Joyce Blazek and Kathleen Gagnon whose ideas, suggestions, and recommendations were invaluable in putting the final touches on the manuscript of *Cloverleaf;* to Shirley D. Ratisseau, my advisor and friend; to my wife, Linda, an English teacher who made sure all of the words were spelled right and all of the commas put in their proper place; and to my son, Josh, for just being around when I got tired of writing.

PROLOGUE

The big red colt screamed in fury, rearing back on his hind legs, his hooves frantically fighting the air as he desperately tried to unloose the thin, frail girl who clung to his back. She grabbed his flaxen mane, buried her face in his thick, muscular neck, and held on as the sorrel bolted madly across the open prairie and on toward the foothills that loomed forbiddingly in the distance.

The battle had begun.

The big horse bucked once, then again, leaping across a narrow, crooked arroyo, veering sharply into a stand of mesquites, doing everything in his power to rid himself of the unwanted rider. The girl refused to fall.

Her back hurt, and the mesquite branches stung her freckled face as they whipped against her without mercy. Her insides were jarred with every step he took, and she felt herself being pitched forward, slipping on the lathered sweat of the sorrel's glistening coat. But she dug her knees into his side and tightened her grip.

She could be just as stubborn as the colt.

To her, it seemed as though the duel would never end.

Then suddenly the big sorrel relaxed, threw his head back, and stretched out in a dead run, his feet flying as though they were trying to outdistance the wind itself. He had torn the reins loose from the girl's hands, and the countryside rushed past her eyes, a ragged blur of color that had neither shape nor form.

She had not conquered the horse. Perhaps no one ever would.

But she had his respect, and, together they ran as one beneath a cloudless Texas sky.

The tall, slender man was smiling proudly as girl and horse, at last, trotted back toward his gray pickup truck. She slid from the sorrel's back, tied him to a mesquite, and ran toward her father.

"I've never gone so fast before," she yelled.

"You had me worried there for a while," the tall, slender man admitted as he hugged her. "He's a rebellious cuss."

"But he runs like the wind."

"What are you gonna name him?"

"I think I'll call him Rebel," she said.

"Why?"

"Because that's what he is."

The man nodded. "I think," he said slowly, "that's what both of you are."

"Then we belong together."

1

Barbara Atkins suddenly felt very alone. She slid off the back of her big sorrel quarterhorse and began climbing the weather-worn chute gate, wiping away the August sweat that had stained her small and freckled face. Her tightly braided pigtails fell limply across her shoulders.

It was obvious that Barbara's blue-checked shirt had been run through the wringer one too many times. The color had faded, and the buttonholes were frayed and no iron had touched it for a long time. She kicked the dust and straw from the soles of her brown calfskin boots and turned her eyes toward the crowded parking lot, searching for the old gray rattletrap pickup truck her father drove. It was nowhere to be seen, and the day was getting late.

Barbara glanced at the clock on the concession stand

wall. She knew that time was running out, that she would be riding soon. She had never before tackled the barrels when her father wasn't in the stands.

James Atkins always sat in the same place, SECTION D, ROW ONE, SEAT FOUR. That put him right behind the first barrel, down close to the arena floor where he could see the grit and determination etched on his daughter's thirteen-year-old face as she and the big sorrel rode hell-bent-for-leather around the cloverleaf pattern that had been stretched out across the sandy, Texas dirt.

The first barrel was the money barrel. Critical seconds, even hundredths of a second, were won or lost depending on how fast horse and rider could reach it and cut sharply around it before dashing madly toward the second barrel. There could be no hesitation, no room for error, especially in a racing event where a single second sometimes separated the top half dozen riders.

The first barrel divided the winners from the losers, the great horses from the good ones, the strong riders from the weak ones. So James Atkins always sat in the same place, a broad grin lighting up his tired face, full of hope and encouragement for the young girl who was now his only reason for living. He was her good luck charm, the strength she needed when the competition got rough, and it was never easy anymore.

"I don't know if I could ride at all if you weren't there to see me," Barbara had told her father late one night as they walked from the small barn behind their white, wooden frame house.

"You don't have to worry," he had assured her.

"Why not?"

"Barbara," her daddy had said softly, "there's nothing on earth that could keep me out of that arena when you're trying to outrun the clock."

"I'm always afraid your job will keep you away," she had replied. "After all, you spend all day driving most of six counties around here."

"I won't let it."

"But what if you're late?"

Atkins grinned and hugged her tightly. "Have I ever been late?" he had asked.

"No, sir."

He had paused a moment and glanced out across the sprawling countryside, watching a cloud slip across the moon. A tiny shadow fell across the Holman's windmill just beyond a barbed wire fence.

"Honey," Atkins had said, "out in this part of Texas, the land is flat, and the roads are straight, and God don't build nothin' but pickup trucks that'll run flat out, and I got one of 'em. When you and Ol' Rebel stretch out toward that first barrel, you can bet that I'll be there yellin' for you."

Barbara had smiled and put her face against his arm. His shirt always smelled of feed and hay. It was a comforting smell. She clung to him in the darkness like a raggedy doll that was always afraid of being misplaced and lost again.

The August sun now pierced her back like a thin-bladed knife, and the salt from her own sweat began to

3

burn her eyes. Barbara rubbed her hands against her blue-checked shirt to dry them, then looked again at SECTION D, ROW ONE, SEAT FOUR.

It was empty.

She felt very much alone, and the knot of nervous butterflies in her stomach ached as though someone had kicked her.

James Atkins was in a hurry, and it seemed he was the only one who cared. His day had started off badly, then began to deteriorate. Hap Woodley, up in Farmer's Grove, hadn't been able to pay for his weekly shipment of feed. He blamed it on the drought that had gripped the heart of West Texas.

"Cattlemen are selling off their herds," he had said. "They don't need much feed anymore, and when the cattlemen aren't buying, I'm not buying either." At the old crossroads store, Atkins found out that Archibald Henry's mother was sick. He figured he must have wasted a good hour and a half just sitting in the breezeway of the old store, waiting for Archibald to get back to work.

When Archibald returned, he complained, "The doctor ain't got time for old people. He was too busy over at the hospital delivering newborns. I guess he just expects the old folks to die off and make room for 'em."

About two hours out of Caprock, James Atkins heard the sickening noise of a tire when it blows and tosses stripped threads of rubber all over the road. His jack was rusty and too cranky to work, and his spare tire had gone flat. He walked three miles down the narrow, dusty road

4

before a work truck full of migrant laborers picked him up and carried him on into Spur.

The laborers were hot, and hadn't bathed since wading across the Rio Grande. And Atkins quickly discovered there wasn't enough room for him to sit upwind from any of them.

He nodded, and they nodded. He smiled, and they smiled. And the truck's driver charged him the last five dollars he had tucked away in his wallet.

Lafe Johnson, down at the Conoco station, let him have a worn-out tire on credit, even sent his younger brother out to drive Atkins some twelve odd miles back down the ranch road to where the old pickup truck sat waiting amidst the mesquite thorns and caliche rock.

"Now, that tire ain't much good," Lafe had told him. "It won't get you far."

"It'll get me home," Atkins said as he wiped the sweat and feed sack dust from his face.

"Maybe," Lafe answered, "Maybe not." He paused a moment, then added, "If it lasts long enough for you to get back up this way, James, you can pay me for it."

Now Atkins was dragging the last ten-pound sack of feed from the bed of his pickup truck and dropping it onto the wooden front porch of Ed Murphy's general store. He stopped to catch his breath and looked quickly up at the clock in the bank window across the street. He didn't like what he saw. Time had gotten away from him. He shook his head. Time had run off and left him.

Murphy scratched his white beard as he checked his inventory list for the last time. He removed his bifocals, rubbed them against his britches leg, then ambled down the steps toward James Atkins. "You want me to write out a check or pay you in cash?" he asked.

"Either one's fine, Ed," Atkins replied, rolling down the sleeves of a white shirt that had become yellow with stain and mildew. "But if you don't mind, I'll just pick it up on my way through here next week."

"Whatcha in such a gosh-durn hurry for?"

Atkins smiled. "My little girl's barrel racin' this afternoon," he said, "an' I'm runnin' awfully late."

Murphy leaned against the unpainted corner post of his store, shaking his head in disbelief. "James, you ain't gonna get nowhere on time in that rattletrap truck you're drivin'."

Atkins shrugged, relieved that his last stop of the day was behind him. "It may not be new," he told the store owner, "but I got it paid for before the tires all fell off, and it'll flat run when I kick it." He jerked the cab door open and climbed in behind the steering wheel. The truck rumbled to a start, throwing gravel as it spun away from Murphy's front porch, limping and bouncing toward the highway.

Murphy shoved his bifocals into his shirt pocket and mumbled mostly to himself, "Shoot, I've seen junkyards in better condition."

Barbara sat perched upon the chute gates, her sorrel tied to the post beside her. The stands had begun filling about four o'clock, and she knew that by now downtown Caprock would be virtually deserted. The stores all

6

closed on Fridays in August when the barrel horses ran.

Caprock had long been a ranching community, wedged into the mesquite and juniper covered brakes, out among the ragged canyons and defiant hills that rose up and leveled off across the high plains of Texas. The land was creased with dry arroyos, wrinkled with age, and as stubborn as those who came to coax a living out of its alkaline dirt. It would be parched one day and flooded the next, depending entirely on the whims of the weather, which no one in his right mind ever tried to predict or second guess.

"How much rain do y'all get out here in a year," a stranded motorist had once asked James Atkins as the two men tried to jump a little life back into a dead battery.

"Oh, about twelve inches."

"That's not much."

"No," Atkins had replied dryly. "But you ought to be here the day it all falls."

In that rugged, isolated stretch of southwestern brush country, only the strong managed to hold on and survive for very long. The weak stayed only long enough to find the road out of town. The cowards never bothered to come at all.

About all the folks in Caprock really had to be proud of was their independence, their horses and, most of all, their kids. On Friday afternoons they gathered down at the rodeo grounds, crowding into wooden bleachers that had been stained gray by the rains and blistered by a summer sun, watching as their daughters and their horses threaded those barrels with the grace of a ballet dancer

7

and the power of a boxer, racing against the wind, the clock, and each other.

The August heat swelled up from the ground around her, and Barbara again rubbed her hands against her blue-checked shirt to dry them, then looked over her shoulder at Kathy Turner, sitting astride a buckskin gelding, staring eagerly ahead, her quirt clenched tightly between her teeth.

The gravel voice of Red Henke boomed over the public address system:

Come a runnin' when you're ready, Miss Kathy.

An expectant hush fell over the crowd, and the gelding burst through the gate as the Caprock High School Band jumped into the middle of a John Philip Sousa march, played slightly faster than ragtime and mostly out of breath. Kathy took the first barrel a little wide, leaning low in the saddle and urging her mount back across the arena floor. The band picked up the frantic rhythm of the horse's hooves themselves, the bass drum throbbing and pounding as the big buckskin swung into the second barrel, almost knocking it over, costing the grim-faced little girl an extra ten precious seconds.

Barbara held her breath, watching the red barrel rock to one edge, spin, then settle back into the dirt. She wanted to win. She would fight hard to win. But Barbara never liked to see any of her friends beat themselves. All she wanted to do was outride them.

After all, that's what competition was all about, and if she didn't make any serious mistakes, she knew that nobody could catch Rebel. He simply refused to lose. He

8

was in a class by himself, an orphan colt nobody had wanted, sold in a two-bit, shadetree auction that had drawn few people and even fewer dollars. Yet Rebel had speed running through his veins, and he could turn on a dime and leave a nickle behind for change. His bloodline wasn't impressive, but his heart was. Rebel would do anything the tiny girl on his back asked him to do; go as fast as she needed to go to win.

Andy Beck, the young county agent who had found herself in charge of the Youth Rodeo Association in Caprock, once told Barbara, "All you can ever hope for is to have one good barrel horse in a lifetime. And you've already gotten yours."

Barbara smiled, glanced quickly at the sorrel standing patiently at her side, then turned again toward the arena. The roar from the stands was growing louder, more feverish, as Kathy cleared the third barrel in the cloverleaf pattern, her face buried in the flying mane of the buckskin. He stormed toward the finish line, urged onward by a brassy blast of voices and trumpets, stomping feet and snare drums that rose up like thunder, waiting for the lightning to strike. Kathy reached for her quirt and slapped it twice against the buckskin's right flank as he dashed past the electric timer and disappeared out the gate into the empty stockyard.

And that high-flyin' run gives little Miss Kathy Turner a time of eighteen point two, Henke announced through the static of his timeworn public address system.

And it moves her into the top ten qualifiers for the West Texas State Barrel Racing Championship and that

9

brand new saddle that goes along with it.

Henke removed his tobacco-stained straw hat and wiped the sweat from his face with a wrinkled red bandana, then continued.

We'd like to pause right here and thank Arnold Edwards down at Arnold's Feed Store for donatin' that silver-studded saddle. Some little lady's gonna be ridin' mighty tall in it just as soon as we get this season behind us.

Henke leaned back in his chair, bit off another plug of Red Man chewing tobacco and grinned at Andy Beck as she bolted up the steps and into the announcer's booth. Her face had been tanned golden by the sun, a symbol of too many hours during too many days out in the blistering heat of the Texas ranching country. She was slender, always in a hurry, only about ten years out of college. Andy had a smile, Red Henke always swore, that would stop a man dead in his tracks and make him break out in a sweat even on a winter day. Her ponytail bounced lightly off her shoulders, and it was the color of the sun itself. Her jeans were faded, her python skin boots scuffed, and her silken western-style shirt was a bright red, tempered somewhat by the dust that had boiled up from the arena floor.

Andy leaned over the scorer's table and told Henke, "Lisa's having trouble with her cinch. So let's make a change in the program. Gloria will run next, then Kimberly."

The gravel-voiced announcer nodded and winked, his heavy-jowled face red with perpetual sunburn. Nothing

10

ever seemed to bother Henke. At the rodeo grounds, he had been the man behind the microphone for as long as anyone could remember. In fact, most of the women with babies in Caprock, and even a few grandmothers, had fond memories of hearing the booming cadence of Henke back during the days when they circled the barrels every weekend. He accepted last minute changes as easily as he accepted a free meal, which he did often down at Hayes Cafe.

Barbara climbed down from the chute gate as the roar of the crowd ushered the next rider toward the first barrel. The band attacked John Philip Sousa again, but she paid no attention. She led Rebel slowly toward the parking lot, her eyes eagerly searching for the sight of her father's battered gray pickup truck. It was nowhere to be seen.

Barbara felt hot. She knew it couldn't be the sun. It was already dropping low in the sky, casting tall shadows from short scrub oak trees. She felt nervous, but knew it couldn't be the race. She had been running the barrels for most of the last six years, ever since she was big enough for her father to sit her in a saddle. The Friday afternoon races were her life, her one chance to excel. Her last chance, she sometimes thought, to be somebody important in Caprock. People had never gone out of their way to speak to her until she and Rebel began winning. Now she was invited to numerous places and events by people she didn't even know. She had never been scared of the barrels. So why did she feel frightened? And lost. And alone.

The big sorrel paused long enough to munch from a pile of scattered hay in the packed-dirt parking lot. From behind her, Barbara heard the noise of the crowd and the band growing louder. She could picture Gloria and her three-year-old roan dashing madly back down the arena floor, reaching and stretching and lunging wildly for the invisible finish line of the electronic timer, running wide open like a lop-eared jackrabbit trying to beat a blue norther home.

At the moment though, she was concerned with neither Gloria nor her horse's time. Her mind was on a gray pickup truck, a hole in its muffler, and the gentle, laughing man who drove it. He had never been this late before. Barbara frowned into the sun, whose broken rays glittered among the scrub oak leaves like drops of gold-plated dew.

When Ricky Rodriguez, the thin, lanky son of the county sheriff, came running through the parked cars, it startled her, and she jumped.

"You nervous?" he asked.

"A little."

Ricky leaned over to stuff his faded jeans back into his water buffalo-hide boots. He was fourteen, and his hat, with a long, ragged turkey feather stuck in the rattlesnake band, had the definite crease of a bull rider.

He grinned. "Don't worry about Gloria," Ricky said matter-of-factly. "She can't catch you. None of'em can. They've all been chasin' Rebel and chewin' his dust all year."

Barbara reached up and patted her big horse's neck,

12

saying, "Rebel doesn't have any use for second place."

She looked up as Andy Beck, hastily glancing at her clipboard, walked quickly toward her.

"You about ready, Barb?" Andy called.

"Just show her the way to the barrels," Ricky yelled with a grin, "then duck or get out of the way."

Andy nodded, put a hand on Barbara's shoulder, and said, "Looks like that championship saddle's as good as in your barn if you can keep from knocking over any of the barrels."

Barbara didn't respond.

"Nobody's beaten you yet," Andy said.

"Nobody's beaten Rebel yet," Barbara corrected her. "Me, I just hang on."

"Yeah," Ricky teased, "if Rebel could sign his name on the entry blank, he wouldn't need Barb at all."

Barbara stuck out her tongue and slugged him on the arm. Andy laughed as she turned to walk away. Barbara's words stopped her.

"Andy," she called, "have you seen my dad out here yet?"

"No." Her eyes, too, glanced quickly over the parking lot, and her smile faded. "But then, I've been running too much to really know who's here."

"He's been delivering feed up around Waco all week," Barbara answered, the spirit gone from her voice. "He said he would be here if he didn't blow a gasket."

"Maybe you've just overlooked him."

"His seat's empty."

Andy walked back to Barbara and put a comforting

13

arm around her. "I'll tell you what, Barb," she said cheerfully, "I'll keep my eyes open for your dad, and you just keep your eyes on the barrels."

The thirteen-year-old nodded and tried to be cheerful again, but the smile never made it to her eyes. The glow of the late-afternoon sun chased the freckles from the dim shadows of her worried face.

James Atkins, chewing hard on a splintered toothpick, settled back in the worn, plaid seats of his pickup truck, keeping his tired eyes on the narrow, graveled road that wound precariously through the high country. He was driving much too fast for a roadway that clung dangerously to the slopes of a steep mountainside and he knew it. But he had a lot of time to make up. James Atkins had taken chances before. His daughter was depending on him. She was waiting on him. He edged the accelerator a little closer to the floor, urging a little more speed out of an engine that had seemingly gone its last mile, but hadn't yet given up the ghost.

Barbara was all he had left in the world, not counting the old rent house where they slept at night, or the pickup truck that sometimes took him where he needed to go and usually got him back home again. She had been only two days old when he lost her mother. Childbirth had been more than his tiny, fragile wife could handle. The doctor had told them to expect complications. But it was a minister who read the last words and a gravedigger who separated him from the only woman he had ever loved.

James Atkins had tried to be a mother to the baby girl,

14

even though he had been too young to even know how to act like a father, which should have come much more naturally. But he managed, and the two of them survived quite nicely. He was on the road a lot, but he could always depend on Andy Beck to keep an eye on Barbara while he was away. Andy knew a lot about horses. She knew a lot more about girls. She had almost become family.

Atkins had no regrets about fatherhood. He had seen the girl take her first step, heard her say her first word, and he enjoyed her laughter when he came home at night. He had bandaged her knee the first time she skinned it, shared her first snow cone on a hot summer day, listened to her read from her first book, taught Barbara her first bedtime prayer. He had watched as she rode her first horse, cried when she won her first barrel race. Atkins hadn't missed much in his daughter's life that counted, and he was bound and determined not to be late anytime that she and Rebel were running the barrels.

He sighed, squinted at the road as the low angle of the sun bounced a sharp reflection off the pickup's hood, almost blinding him. He slowly turned the knob on his radio, searching for KTRY, his hometown radio station, lost somewhere between the static and George Jones's latest hit. At last he heard the unmistakable voice of Charlie Gasway, a part-time disc jockey who had made a career of broadcasting any event that took place out at the rodeo grounds.

It was seventeen minutes after five, and Barbara should be running soon, unless, of course, there had been a lot of delays, and Atkins prayed there had been.

Sweat curled down his back and it wasn't from the heat. Barbara must be worried now, he thought. He had never been this late before. She expected him to watch her run the barrels, and he had never let her down.

Atkins rubbed his face and turned his truck into the sun as it began crawling down into the brakes behind the splintered juniper and prickly pear, leaving pink and charcoal shadow in its wake. As he topped the hill, Atkins jammed the accelerator harder on the floor, and a tire blew with the sudden sound of a distant shotgun blast.

The speeding pickup truck twisted out of control, jerking him loose from the steering wheel. Frantically, he reached back, grabbed the wheel again and cut back sharply to the left. The pickup shuddered as if it would break, then pitched onto its side as Charlie Gasway was announcing,

As you know, we got big doin's out at the fairgrounds today, with some of the cutest little hometown girls you ever saw competin' for the Barrel Racin' Championship.

The truck spun wildly and crashed through the guard rail, tumbling end-over-end down amongst the rocks on the mountainside, a movement that seemed agonizingly slow and deliberate, as torn metal ground and scraped its way toward the bed of a dry arroyo, slamming at last into an old, gnarled oak tree and coming to rest in a cloud of caliche dust.

The engine coughed once and died. Atkins lay slumped against the steering wheel, his eyes closed, his arms hanging limply at his side. The charcoal gray of the afternoon shadows gently touched his face, and the

16

silence was broken only by the radio voice of Charlie Gasway.

...So, if Albert's figurin' is right, at the halfway point, we got no changes at all in the top four places. So the race is on for all the marbles, and, I'll tell you, I'd rather try to predict the weather than pick a winner out there.

A blue-headed chaparral cock darted from the cactus and raced across the rippled sand of the arroyo. The wind covered its tracks as though it had never been there. A strange calm fell with the shadows across the land.

Barbara Atkins left the parking lot and with Rebel ambled back toward the arena as Kimberly Hampton rounded the final barrel and charged, amidst the tumult of the band's brass section, toward the finish line. The day hadn't cooled any. Temperatures were still on the hot side of one hundred degrees. Barbara felt clammy and cold, and she didn't know why.

Ricky Rodriguez, hurrying from the concession stand, handed her a hot dog with mustard dripping from the bun. He saw her shiver slightly and asked, "You gettin' butterflies?"

Barbara shrugged. "A few."

In the background, at the scorer's table Red Henke was continuing,

A good time of nineteen point three for little Miss Kimberly Hampton, ridin' that big gray ropin' horse of

18

*her daddy's. Comin' up next we have Juanita Madrone's
daughter, Lisa, who comes into this next-to-the-last race
of the year in fourth place, only a second and a half out of
third. With a good run, she's got a doggone good chance
of grabbin' herself a trophy.*

Barbara tied Rebel to the gate, then she and Ricky
scrambled to the top rail of the wooden fence that
encircled the arena. Again she glanced at SECTION D,
ROW ONE, and SEAT FOUR. It was still empty.

Ricky wiped mustard off his chin with the back of his
hand, grinned, and taunted Barbara, "Well, at least you
don't fall off near as often as you used to."

"That's when I had an old plow horse that stopped
everytime he came to a barrel," she answered in her own
defense.

"Yeah. He'd stop and you wouldn't."

"If you think it's easy," Barbara said sharply, "you
ought to ride the barrels."

"I'd rather ride bulls."

"Bulls don't like you."

Ricky grinned. "Neither do the barrels," he said.

"Bulls'll try to run over you," Barbara told him bluntly.

"They have to throw me first."

"And just how did you lose those two front teeth?"

Ricky choked down the last of his hot dog, wiped his
hands on his denim vest, and admitted, "He threw me
first and kicked me second."

Barbara laughed. It was the best she had felt all day.
"Well," she said, all prim and proper, "I want you to
know that I have never been thrown, kicked, or attacked

19

by an angry barrel."

"Maybe not," Ricky replied, the smile fading from his face, "but, Barb, you've got more troubles than I have."

"What do you mean?"

He nodded over his shoulder, and Barbara's eyes followed his gaze. She saw Sharon Wilson riding her dark chestnut barrel horse slowly across the parking lot, sitting straight and regal in the saddle, looking very much out of place among the dust-splattered pickup trucks that blocked her way. Barbara had always thought that Sharon was the most beautiful girl she had ever seen, almost perfect. She had long, black hair that framed an oval face, with jet black eyes and olive skin that had no blemishes at all. She was fifteen and looked older. That, perhaps, was why Barbara envied her. Her face wasn't sprinkled liberally with freckles, and that, for sure, was why Barbara disliked her.

Sharon Wilson sometime resembled a high-fashion mannequin at Neiman-Marcus, which was the only place she would dare buy her clothes. She never liked to wear the same outfit twice during the barrel racing season. She didn't have to. Her father owned the largest spread in the county, and he had become one of the wealthiest, most influential men in West Texas, even venturing into banking when the everyday operation of running a quarterhorse ranch began to bore him. He was a quiet man, soft spoken, and dedicated to the whims and wishes of his daughter. What she wanted, she got, and she always wanted a lot. Money was no object.

"I've worked hard for the success I've had," he liked to

say, "and it doesn't do a man any good to have a few dollars unless he has somebody important to spend it on." Warren P. Wilson had his daughter Sharon.

Sharon stood in the saddle as the wind gently brushed the hair from her face, frowning, uncomfortable in the whirling dervish of sand that blew helter-skelter across the parking lot. Her matching yellow shirt and pants were obviously the handiwork of some New York designer who had never been West, and flashing silver sequins seemed to attract the late afternoon sun like tiny magnets.

The chestnut wanted to run, but Sharon kept holding him back. He always wanted to run, but then, he had speed and endurance bred into his high-priced blood. The trouble was, he lost precious time circling the barrels, and that made him a critical step or two too slow, and Sharon had spent the whole season with first place just a fraction beyond her frantic grasp.

She wanted to win. It was an obsession. Wilsons never accepted second place, especially in their own hometown. That would be a disgrace. Those times when Sharon lost, she blamed the chestnut. She would also go for days without speaking to her father.

Barbara stared at Sharon, and she felt hollow, a peasant in the presence of royalty.

Suddenly her jeans seemed more faded than before. She tried to hide the hole that peeked through the leather sole of her boot, and she hated her common, ordinary, everyday brown hair. The freckles across her nose began to itch, or at least she thought they did.

The chestnut looked faster than ever. Sharon scowled,

and the sequins glittered as though they were diamonds.

"Sharon wants the championship real bad," Barbara said to Ricky. "And she's used to gettin' what she wants."

Ricky shrugged and tilted the front of his hat down lower over his eyes. "Sharon's just greedy, that's all," he answered. "She's already got all the money in the world and most of what's in Caprock. What her daddy ain't got, he can flat get."

"That's what scares me."

"Don't worry," Ricky told her. "Money can't buy a championship."

"I hope not."

"But if it can," Ricky said, grinning, "my money's on Rebel."

"How much you got?"

"I only lack a dollar and a half havin' forty-seven cents."

Barbara laughed again, watching Sharon Wilson ride briskly toward a big horse trailer parked away from the pickup trucks and hitched onto the back of a long, sleek, black Cadillac. A sign on the side of the sky blue trailer advertised,

WARREN P. WILSON ENTERPRISES
WILSON RANCH AND STUD FARM
HOME OF *LUCKY DIAMOND*

Wilson, dressed in a tailored dark-gray western suit, expensive ostrich-hide boots, and a white Stetson, stepped away from the trailer to meet his daughter. His broad smile was filled with pride, and he reached up to help Sharon dismount, lightly kissing her cheek as her feet touched the ground. She quickly wiped the kiss away.

Atop the arena fence, Barbara rolled her eyes in disgust, or maybe it was jealousy. Sharon was the one obstacle standing between her and that championship saddle. Sharon had a horse from the best bloodlines in Texas. And Sharon's father was standing by her side, holding her, supporting her, providing a strong, gentle arm to lean on. Barbara again cast a quick, nervous glance at SECTION D, ROW ONE, SEAT FOUR. Still, it was empty.

Ricky, his nose in the air, reached up and mimicked Wilson's stiff, stuffy, almost formal method of taking his daughter's hand. He thought he could make Barbara laugh. This time, he was wrong.

Wilson, with affection, placed his arm around his daughter's shoulder, and walked with her toward the awaiting arena. His young foreman, Grady Wyatt, ambled slowly behind, chewing casually on a straw and leading the chestnut. His hat and boots were those of a working man, stained with sweat and speckled with tobacco juice. He was lean and hard, more at home in the saddle than on foot, and the wrinkles in the corners of his eyes were always threatening to break out in an embarrassed grin.

Wilson looked down at Sharon and said softly, "Just turn old Diamond Cutter loose out there, sweetheart. I love to watch you run. Makes a real pretty sight for these old eyes of mine."

Sharon nodded. She took her number from Andy Beck

23

and quickly mounted the chestnut, clenching the quirt between her teeth and adjusting her riding gloves. She didn't bother to look at her father as he walked to her side, reached up, and squeezed her hand for good luck. "Just give it your best shot, sweetheart," he called loudly.

"That's never good enough," Sharon snapped. "I'd have better luck if you got me a better horse."

Wilson forced a smile. "You'll be a winner," he encouraged her. "I know you will. Your time's coming."

"My time's running out, and I don't like it." Sharon's voice was filled with both self-pity and disgust. "You know what it takes to win." The girl squeezed her words out slowly, and they were hardened with resentment. "Get it."

Sharon looked up as she heard Red Henke call her name over the public address system. She removed her hand from her father's grasp.

Currently in second place, Henke announced, *only six point four seconds out of first place is Miss Sharon Wilson astride Diamond Cutter. She's certainly got a good shot at the West Texas Championship, and she's up next. Come a runnin' anytime you're ready Miss Sharon.*

The tall black-haired girl leaned forward in the saddle, slapped the chestnut sharply with the knotted end of her leather quirt, and Diamond Cutter bolted forward and charged out into the arena. Wilson propped himself up against the gate, never taking his eyes off her, and the smile was gone from his face. Worry creased the wrinkles on his forehead, then anger. He spoke to Grady without turning around, his eyes masked with disappointment.

24

"If she loses, it's all my fault," he said. "Sharon can't win ridin' a second-class horse."

Grady simply shook his head. "Then that's gotta be the most expensive second-class horse in Texas," he drawled. "He was sired by Lucky Diamond himself."

"Lucky Diamond was better at racing than breeding."

"He's fast."

"Not fast enough."

"He's just a three-year-old," Grady argued. "Give him a chance to learn what he's supposed to be doin'. You know as well as I do, Mr. Wilson, that it takes several good years of trainin' before a horse feels comfortable turnin' the barrels."

"I don't have the luxury of time," Warren Wilson said, his voice low, his words frantic. "Sharon's only got another year or two before she's too old for the barrels. She wants to win, and she wants to win now. Grady, I'm afraid that I can't afford to wait. By then, it'll be too late."

Grady shrugged. When Wilson had made up his mind about something, he knew, there was no use trying to change it. He was a good man, but a stubborn man. He had money and he had prestige. He generally had the right connections in the right places. If Wilson wanted something, he got it. Sometimes he bought it. Sometimes he took it. At any rate, nobody ever had enough gall to step forward and tell him he couldn't have it. Grady sure didn't. He liked eating too well. He liked a roof over his head. Most of all, he liked those weekly paychecks.

Sharon and Diamond Cutter thundered past them in a shower of dust, and at the microphone the voice of Henke was booming,

A brilliant time of sixteen point seven for Miss Sharon Wilson. That's the fastest time of the day, and the second fastest time of the year. Great ride, honey.

So it was. Wilson, having found his smile again, ran to her side and hugged her in triumph as she dismounted. The sequins reached out and caught the sun, lighting up like neon. But not even the sun could chase the shadows from her face.

"I knew you could do it," Wilson said proudly. "I told you Diamond Cutter would make you a champion."

"He slowed down on the last barrel." Her voice was cold and grating.

"But you had a time of sixteen point seven," her father told her. "That's tremendous, Sharon."

Sharon walked away from the chestnut, brushing that long, black hair from her face. She stopped for a moment and nodded toward Barbara, leading Rebel past the concession stand and on toward the gate.

"She's gone faster," Sharon said curtly. "Maybe if I had her horse, I could go faster, too."

She wheeled around and pushed her way through the crowd, leaving her father with a pained expression cutting across his face. He sighed. Grady took the chestnut's reins, and the two men walked in silence back toward the black Cadillac.

Barbara held the number that Andy Beck handed her, grinned a nervous grin, and wiped away the sweat and dust mixed together in the corner of her eyes.

"Have you seen daddy yet?" she asked.

Andy shook her head.

"I've looked everywhere," Barbara told her.

Andy hoped that her smile would somehow reassure the tiny, freckle-face girl, but she doubted it.

Without another word, Barbara grabbed the saddle horn and pulled herself onto the broad back of the big sorrel. As she rode away, she heard the raw squeal of tires as they left the pavement and tore into the dirt parking lot at high speed.

It must be some smart-aleck high school bull rider showing off in his daddy's pickup, she thought. Or it could be her father. He was running late, and he would definitely be in a hurry. Barbara stood in the stirrups, turned, and saw the sheriff's car come bouncing up along the row of pickup trucks, almost hidden in the dust that exploded upward from beneath the vehicle. Disappointed, she seated herself in the saddle again and waited to hear Red Henke call her name. She was as ready as she would ever be, and Rebel was always eager to run.

Ricky Rodriguez had just given Andy a wrinkled cup of Coca-Cola when he saw his father's patrol car slide to a stop. He grinned at Andy. "I haven't seen Daddy in that big a hurry since I turned the pigs loose," he said.

Sheriff Rodriguez, his face solemn, opened the door, spotted Andy, slipped quickly out from behind the steering wheel, and trotted to her. He removed his dark glasses, gently took her arm and asked, "Where's Barbara?"

"Getting ready to ride. Why?"

"It's her father."

He paused, groping for words.

"He's been in a wreck."

Andy caught her breath. "Oh, Lord, J.T., what happened?"

"He must have been in an awful hurry when the tire blew. There's just not enough road up there to hold onto when you lose control of your car like that."

He paused again and wiped the grime from his face. Then he continued, "James hit the guard rail without ever slowin' down."

"How bad is he?"

"He didn't make it."

Andy and Sheriff Rodriguez turned and looked toward the arena gate as Henke announced:

Closin' out today's program will be your first place leader, Miss Barbara Atkins. She's got her sights on that saddle and swears there ain't nobody gonna take it away from her. Barb, as soon as you and that big sorrel of yours are ready, come a ridin'.

Barbara crouched low in the saddle, determination set deep in her eyes, and Rebel surged forward through the gate. He was a picture of grace and strength, attacking the first barrel as the crowd hushed, and the band played louder and faster, trying to match, or at least catch, the sorrel's long, powerful strides.

Working as one, girl and horse bent sharply around the first barrel and sprinted for the second, lost in the glare of a dust screen, shaving it close. A quiet, expectant roar rose from the throat of the crowd. Rebel pointed for the last barrel, Barbara whispered and shouted and urged him to full speed, her body perfectly synchronized to the pounding rhythm of the muscular horseflesh beneath her. The sorrel flared a shade wide, then bolted for the finish line, the sound of his hoofbeats swallowed up by the cheering and a brass trumpet overture. Rebel blasted past the electronic timer and the announcer Henke, his voice hoarse, was shouting,

Unbelievable. A sixteen point six. Still undefeated. A championship may be just one ride away for little Miss Barbara Atkins.

Barbara, filled with elation, jumped to the ground beside Ricky and hugged her horse, caught up in the spirit of triumph and jubilation. The day belonged to her, and, of course, to Rebel. Sharon had a good time, maybe even a great time, she thought. But she, Barbara, had better. So what if she didn't have a yellow outfit with silver sequins or long black hair. It didn't matter. Not really. Not now anyway. She hugged Rebel again and looked up at Ricky.

"Did my dad ever get here?" she asked. "He would have been real proud of Rebel today."

Ricky didn't answer. He felt awkward, uncomfortable, out of place. He couldn't even look his best friend in the eyes, and he hated himself for it. He turned away.

"You just can't trust gaskets," Barbara said.

Barbara found herself surrounded by the girls she rode with and against. Lisa Madrone. Gloria Westhaven. Kathy Turner. All reaching to pat her on the back. All shouting. Some wanting to hug her. All glad that she had turned away the challenge of that smart-aleck Sharon Wilson one more time. They were all there, all except Sharon. Barbara grinned broadly, and, for once, she didn't even think about the freckles that usually itched across the bridge of her nose.

"You got the jelly beans?" she called to Ricky.

He nodded, pulling a bag of candy from his pocket and handing it to Barbara. She rummaged around inside the dime store sack and pulled out a couple of black jelly beans, then fed them to her sorrel.

"He likes licorice best," Barbara grinned.

Andy Beck gently pushed her way through the crowd that had gathered around the winning horse and rider. She had no idea what she would say to the girl, but somebody had to tell her. She felt dizzy, nauseous and, for a moment, thought she was either going to pass out or throw up in the dreadful West Texas heat.

"Rebel would win the Kentucky Derby for a licorice jelly bean," Barbara said as Andy reached her side. "Have you ever seen a horse run any better than that?"

Andy shook her head, a forced movement, mechanical with no emotion at all. The young county agent was trying hard to gather the strength it would take to break the news to the little rider, searching in her mind for the right words to say and coming up empty.

Barbara saw that Andy's face was strained, etched with compassion, a shade too gray. Her eyes were blurred, the laughter was gone. She sensed something was wrong, terribly wrong. She had never seen Andy look that way before, and she felt scared. She wanted to run, and she had nowhere to go, and she knew she didn't want to hear what Andy would be telling her, whatever it was.

"He could have run all day," Barbara said, her words coming faster, not wanting to give Andy a chance to talk at all, confused, feeling very much alone, feeling as though she was trapped in a nightmare and wanting to wake up again and knowing that she wouldn't. "He could have run all day and never slowed down and nobody would have ever caught him. You can just feel it when Rebel —"

"Come with me, Barb," Andy softly interrupted her. "I've got to talk to you."

She took the girl's arm and led her away from the crowd until the tumult and the shouting was muffled behind them. The echo of the band seemed far away. Barbara realized she couldn't hear it anymore.

"What's wrong?" she asked.

"There's been an accident, Barb."

Behind them, a stilted hush fell awkardly upon the stands as the news was whispered from person to person.

"My dad?"

"He was hurrying to get back and watch you run."

"He's okay, isn't he?"

"He loved you very much, Barb."

Andy stared down at the girl, and she thought how tiny she looked, how fragile. How unfair life could be sometimes. She reached out and wiped a speck of dirt away from the girl's cheek.

Barbara's eyes moistened, and a tear rolled down her cheek. Somehow, she had known her father wouldn't be

31

coming back, not when SEAT FOUR, ROW ONE, SECTION D had been left empty. She just hadn't wanted to believe the fear that had raged inside of her. There had been hope, always hope, and now there wasn't any anymore. Her face was drawn in anguish and in pain. Andy pulled the girl to her, wrapping her arms around Barbara's trembling shoulders, for a moment closing the world away. Then the flood of tears came, with sobs of despair. She buried her face against Andy's shoulder. The crumpled sack dropped. The jelly beans lay scattered on the ground beside her boots.

An old pickup truck chugged its way along a winding dirt road that led out of the evening shadows and came to rest beside a tall oak tree atop a bald knob overlooking the cemetery. The truck had once been blue, but now it was mostly rust, a survivor that had seen more than its share of hard miles. So had its driver.

Gabriel B. Spencer stepped out into the wind that had bent the oak tree but hadn't yet broken it. His beard was white, his boots aging and sandblasted by the West Texas desert. A black, wrinkled jacket hung haphazardly over his faded jeans. Thick white hair curled down from the bottom of his sweat-stained hat. His red suspenders strained against his belly, and the pinstripes on his shirt had almost been washed away. His face was like leather. the legacy of too many years in a blistering, unforgiving sun. And his fingers were gnarled from working too many roundups at the hind end of a kicking calf at branding time.

Gabriel reached into his left boot, pulled out a crumpled package of chewing tobacco and bit himself off a chew. He scratched his beard, straightened his broad but sagging shoulders, and stared down into the dried garden of wind-chiseled stones. The soil was hallowed to him. It held a lot of his friends, some whose faces he could no longer remember. He had even learned the names of the strangers who now lay in the burying ground.

Then his eyes rested on the expressionless face of a tiny girl with ordinary brown hair and freckles that crept shamelessly across the bridge of her nose.

Barbara, more frail than usual in a loose, black secondhand dress with ruffles on the sleeves, stood awkwardly between Andy Beck and Sheriff J.T. Rodriguez, holding on to the county agent's arm for support. She looked ahead without seeing, her eyes drained of tears. She was numb in the midst of a dream that seemed to have no end. A yellow flower dropped from the small bouquet that Barbara was clutching, but she didn't notice. The wind gently blew it away, out among the gray stones, out where a person's entire life's story could be written in a single line — the date of birth and the date of death.

A small crowd had gathered around the silver metallic casket lying above an open grave. Warren P. Wilson was there, as was Grady Wyatt, Arnold Edwards from down at the feed store, and the parents of several of the barrel racers who had spent almost all summer chasing Barbara across the finish line.

The minister closed his Bible, removed his gold-rimmed spectacles, and looked out at them all. His voice was soft, and the words came easily to him that evening. He had used them so many times before.

"It's sometimes difficult to understand the master plan of God," the preacher said.

Few heard him. Barbara stood in a daze, aware that she was standing beside the grave of her father, not really yet comprehending that he wouldn't be coming back home, jovial as usual, singing *You are my sunshine,* and pitching a bag of cold hamburgers on the kitchen table.

Warren P. Wilson nervously glanced at his watch. He had a political meeting scheduled down at the Democratic headquarters in thirty minutes. However, he had never once thought of missing the funeral of James Atkins. He knew that it was important to be seen anywhere the voters — regardless of how many of them — had gathered together. He might even be running for public office someday soon.

Grady Wyatt had a sick horse that was troubling him. Arnold Edwards needed to get back and close down his store. Hap Hubbard was keeping it open for him, and he didn't like the idea of paying Hap overtime.

All were in a hurry. But all watched the preacher with reverence and solemn faces. They knew when to pay respect, and how to pay it.

The minister continued, "It's hard to understand why such a dear one as James Atkins is taken from us. But one day we shall understand it better when we are all led

35

across that Jordan River together...Let us pray."

The heads bowed, and hats were removed. On top of the bald knob, Gabriel Spencer wiped the sweat from his forehead and nodded his approval, never taking his eyes off the scene that was unfolding below him. The minister's words were barely discernible to him, and he leaned forward to catch what he could of the closing prayer.

Now we stand before you with hearts heavy in grief. But we know that we can always turn to you and you, dear Lord, will dry our eyes and take that burden of grief off our weary shoulders. Thy will be done, oh Lord. Amen.

Gabriel watched as the small crowd parted, and each one went his separate way. Wilson stepped forward to shake Barbara's hand, though he doubted she would ever remember it. Grady smiled at her, and she tried to smile back, but the smile never came, and, embarrassed, she looked away.

The mothers of the barrel racers hugged her, the fathers awkwardly patted her back. Finally, Andy put an arm around Barbara to lead her back to the waiting limousine. Halfway to the road, the small, freckle-faced girl stopped and looked back over her shoulder at the casket. She turned and ran to the graveside and, as a last act of love for her father, she placed the small bouquet of flowers on the silver metallic lid.

Andy patiently waited for her. She looked up at the sheriff and said simply, "She'll be staying on with me. For now anyway."

Rodriguez nodded. "If she needs anything, call us."

"Thanks, Sheriff."

For Barbara, the short distance from the casket of her father to the open doors of the black limousine was the longest walk of her life. The car would drive away, and he would be gone as though he had simply left for work one day and disappeared. And all she had to cling to were memories.

There was the picture in the old trunk, taken only a year ago, shortly after she had won her first race with Rebel. Her father wore the proudest smile of all. She could go downtown and look in the window of Meyers Jewelry Store and see the birthstone ring he had promised to buy her next Christmas. His seed catalogs were the bible that he read at night. The kewpie doll he had won pitching pennies at the county fair hung above her bed. And, of course, out in the corral was the horse he had given her.

Barbara prayed she could find the picture. The painted face of the kewpie doll was smeared and peeling. The seed catalogs had been thrown from the pickup when it rolled down into the juniper brakes, and the wind had scattered them across the prairie. And she was afraid that, with the passing years, the memories would leave her as surely as her father had.

Andy took Barbara's trembling hand and helped her into the limousine. The door slammed shut. Barbara turned, staring hard through the rear window for one last, lingering look as the car pulled away. She didn't see the casket, hidden for a moment behind the brown, thirsty hedges. Her gaze was locked on the unkempt image of an old man in a black hat and a black, wrinkled jacket who was ambling slowly down through weathered cemetery stones to pay his last respects.

Marvin Lockhart, the funeral home director, stood with his assistant, methodically and mechanically preparing to lower the casket into the ground. He heard Gabriel Spencer cough, and the sound startled him. He had thought everyone was gone. He had watched them all drive away, and Marvin Lockhart didn't like to be bothered in the middle of his work.

He turned stoically, his hands clasped in front of him, and looked into the faded blue eyes of the old man.

"Can I be of service to you, sir?"

"Not as long as I'm breathin'," Gabriel snapped.

"I'm sorry, sir, but the funeral has already ended." Marvin's voice was a monotone, low and solemn.

"I know," the old man answered. "It ended years ago."

Gabriel glanced quickly at the silver, metallic casket, then looked down at a much older grave at his feet. His face softened, and the old man removed his hat, bowed his head, and murmured a silent prayer, something about love and honor and pride and sometimes feeling as all alone as a single cloud in a drought-sticken sky. Gabriel suddenly reached over, took a white carnation from the funeral wreath of James Atkins and placed it carefully beside the headstone that read:

Miriam Atkins.
Beloved Wife and Mother.
1940-1968.

He breathed deeply, touched by the sharp, unforgiving pain of old memories, and, for a moment, he could only remember her as a five-year-old girl running down the dirt, country road to meet him in the twilight as he walked home from the fields.

Others that day had come to mourn James Atkins. Gabriel had come to remember his daughter, the woman James Atkins had married and taken from him. He still missed her and always would.

Gabriel, his aging shoulders sagging and his steps weary, slowly began trudging back up the rise toward the bald knob. He would have cried, he guessed. But Gabriel B. Spencer hadn't cried in almost twenty years.

Night slipped quietly across the brakes, and the sun pulled long shadows down through the canyons as it dropped off the face of the earth somewhere just west of Amarillo. Darkness, in August, brought relief. The winds cooled, and the sands no longer simmered with the heat of a desert furnace. Most of Caprock slept.

Barbara couldn't. Dressed in her pale blue nightgown and robe, she slipped out the front door of Andy's small, frame home, and walked out toward the edge of a white picket fence that enclosed the front yard. She ran her right hand over the dull, pointed tips of the hand sawed pickets, stared through the mesquite grove and down the empty roadway that passed the little white cottage. Her face was a mirror of loneliness.

In the distance she heard the faraway whine of an approaching car. Her eyes widened hopefully, and Barbara leaned forward, straining against the fence, waiting, wondering, praying, as the harsh glare of the headlights struck her across the face. It was a pickup truck. Was it gray? Did it have seed catalogs scattered in the back seat? Was that someone singing, *You are my sunshine?* Could it be?

The red and black pickup truck rumbled on past without slowing down, and Barbara, holding the white picket so tightly her hands trembled, watched it until the red taillights had turned the corner at James Fincher's Shell Station and vanished. Aching with disappointment, Barbara buried her forehead against the back of her hands, dropped to her knees, and waited for the morning to come and chase the darkness away.

Inside her bedroom, Andy Beck yawned and stretched, waking from a fitful sleep. She picked up the electric clock from the nightstand and its hands, glowing in the dark, told her it was two-thirty. Andy felt rotten. A dull throb pounded the back of her head, and her eyes scratched as though someone had thrown sand into them. Her bedcovers were wet with sweat, and she wasn't sure that she had slept much at all.

Andy replaced the clock and glanced around the room, realizing that the pallet beside her bed was empty. Alarmed, she scrambled out of bed, grabbed her robe off the back of an antique rocking chair, and draped it around her shoulders. She walked quickly across the room and toward the front door. It was open, and a thin blade of moonlight had sliced its way into the house.

Andy found Barbara, still leaning against the fence, her chin propped up on folded arms. An easterly wind ruffled her hair, and the gnarled branches of the mesquite thicket shaded her face from a prying moon. Barbara heard footsteps and looked up to see Andy moving down the sidewalk toward her.

"I'm having trouble sleeping myself," Andy said softly. "It must be the heat...and the gnats."

Barbara nodded and stared back down that long, empty road.

"I keep thinking daddy may still be out there delivering feed somewhere," she said. "That he's just late getting home." She paused, then continued, "I wake up everytime I hear a pickup coming. I keep thinking that maybe it's him."

Andy sat down beside her. "I'm sorry, Barb. I know it must be awfully hard for you."

"It's just not fair." Anger and bitterness had crept into Barbara's voice. "I never knew my mama. And my daddy's dead. I don't have anybody else in the whole world. What's gonna happen to me?"

Andy stroked the girl's hair to comfort her.

"You've got a home with me, Barb."

Barbara continued to watch the road. She hadn't heard Andy's words. She didn't want to listen. She only wanted to sort out her own feelings, to get a grip on life. She was trying hard to hold on, trying to find something tangible and worthwhile to remember and call her own.

"Daddy bought Rebel for me," she blurted out. "I picked him out myself. But daddy bought him."

"I know."

"He saved every spare dime he could get his hands on.

He needed a new truck, but he just kept fixing up his old one when it broke down. We ate a lot of leftovers until he got enough money to pay for Rebel."

She paused, then smiled.

"Daddy said I fixed leftovers better than anybody he had ever seen," Barbara said.

"He loved you very much."

Barbara stood up straight, and her face darkened. A cloud had stretched out to swallow up the moon, and the north star was the brightest light left in the summertime sky. She watched it in silence, waiting until the cloud broke up and drifted away. *Star light,* she thought. *Star bright.* But there were no wishes to make, none that could come true anyway. The moon had been freed from the gloom, the darkness that had held it. She hadn't been freed, and felt that she never would be.

"Daddy watched me ride in every race I ever had," Barbara said wistfully.

"He was proud of you," Andy whispered. "I saw it in his face every time you rode. He grinned the biggest and yelled the loudest and always hated to see the barrel racing season end worse than you did."

Barbara turned away from the fence. "I bet Rebel's lonesome, too," she said softly.

Andy nodded. She took the girl's hand and together they walked back toward the little white cottage. Andy could feel the temperature changing. The wind was finally cool, and she knew that morning couldn't be far away. The heat would soon be rising again from the prairie floor, dried and cracked and moistened only by the sweat of those who worked upon it.

"Let's try to get us a little more sleep now," Andy said. "Tomorrow will be here before you know it."

Barbara paused just long enough to look one more time down the deserted highway. The words to *You Are My Sunshine* kept running through her head. For the life of her, she couldn't remember the tune.

4

A quarterhorse ran playfully behind the white, wooden fences of the Warren P. Wilson Ranch, the wind blowing casually through its chestnut mane. For a time, he had the northern end of the pasture to himself, far away from the herd still grazing down alongside the banks of Prairie Dog Creek. He slowed to a stop beside the gate, snorted, then bolted toward the mesquite grove under a morning sun still trying to cut its way through a haze of West Texas dust.

Irrigation pipes threw man-made rain onto the pasture, and the grasses remained green even though they had wilted beneath the scorching touch of summer. Fragments of a rainbow were pieced together in the irrigation spray, and a covey of blue quail flushed skyward as the quarterhorse ran into the splintered shade of the mesquite trees.

Slowly, the day was waking up, a hum of quiet voices, an occasional laugh, the throb of a nearby pumping oil rig, and the muffled beat of horses trotting lightly on the parched earth. In the distance, the unmistakable patrol car of Sheriff J.T. Rodriguez pulled off the main road and eased up the long, winding driveway.

Out beside the corral, Gabriel B. Spencer knelt in the dirt beside a white-faced heifer that was straining on the rope that kept her tethered. He gently stroked the cow's neck to calm her, chewing on a cigar he had forgotten to light. His eyes were tired, his shoulders slumped.

Grady had awakened him early that morning, saying the boss man's cattle weren't acting right, and Gabriel never turned his back on a sick cow. "I can cure 'em," he always said, "or I can kill 'em. But I never leave 'em the way they were when I found 'em." Ranchers trusted him, and Gabriel never lost an animal that could be saved.

He wiped the blade of his knife on the leg of his britches and slowly, carefully, began drilling a tiny hole at the base of the heifer's horn. The cow bawled and kicked, angry, perhaps, but not in pain. Grady marveled at how steady the old man's gnarled, aging hands always became when he treated livestock.

"Your cattle's got a bad case of holler horn," the old man said.

"Andy says there ain't no such thing as hollow horn."

Gabriel removed his cigar and pointed it at Grady. "It's just that them book-learned folks have got fancier names for it, that's all. They feel like they can charge you more money if they tell you a cow's got a disease you can't

45

pronounce. But it's all the same. You can pay for some of them high-priced drugs if you want to — but sprinklin' a little salt in the horn'll cure it every time."

"You're not a doctor," Grady told him, kneeling to watch as the tiny grains of salt were funneled into the horn. "How come you know so much about cows?"

Gabriel shrugged. "I've owned a lot of 'em in my time," he said. "I've sold a lot of 'em. I've raised a lot of 'em from calves. And I've watched a lot of 'em die. Over the years, me an' the good Lord have figured out what works most of the time and what works some of the time. And I know when to walk off an' leave 'em alone."

Gabriel stood, and Grady quickly untied the heifer, slapping her on the rump as she scrambled to her feet. The old man picked the straw from his white beard as Sheriff Rodriguez walked into the barn.

"You got a minute, Gabe?" he asked.

"I'm busy."

"I need to talk to you." The sheriff wore a frown.

"I'm listenin'."

"It's a personal matter."

Gabriel knelt again, leaning over another bawling cow, touching her horn with the tip of his knife.

"Talk away, J.T.," he said. "I ain't goin' nowhere."

Rodriguez leaned over Gabriel's shoulder, trying to keep his voice low and confidential, grateful that Grady had had the decency to walk away and leave them alone. "It's about your granddaughter, Gabe," he said. "She's gonna be needin' a home."

Gabriel didn't answer.

46

He continued to clean out the hole, gently blowing the shavings away. His silence left Rodriguez looking uncomfortable, feeling as though he were in an awkward place at an awkward time. The sheriff waited, but Gabriel ignored him.

"You hear me?" Rodriguez finally asked.

"Yup."

"What are you gonna do about it?"

"Nothin'."

"You're the last living relative Barbara has," the sheriff told him, a touch of irritation edging into his voice. "She needs a home."

Gabriel nodded, unconcerned. "I'm sure you can find some nice folks who'll be glad to keep an eye out for her," he replied. "She's a smart little girl. Won't give 'em no trouble at all."

"Maybe you're right." The sheriff's tone softened. "But you're family, Gabe, the only real family she's got left."

Gabriel sighed deeply and turned to face the sheriff. "I've already raised one family," he said. "I'm a little too old to be inheritin' another one now."

"She needs you."

Gabriel took a match stick out of his jacket pocket, quickly whittled out a small peg, and gently shoved it into the hole he had drilled into the heifer's horn.

"All she needs," he said, "is a place with four walls, a roof over her head, a floor beneath her feet, somebody to make sure she gets to school on time and has supper on the table when she gets back to the house. Besides, she probably ain't got no hankerin' at all to move in with an

47

old, over-the-hill, washed up horse doctor."

"Why don't you ask her?"

"Where's she stayin' now?"

"Over at Andy's."

Gabriel grunted, and a frown cut its way deeper into the old man's face, ashen and wrinkled, as gray as a creekbed out in the desert where no rains ever came.

"I wouldn't trust Andy with a head of sick cattle," he muttered, "but she's probably got the hang of lookin' out for little girls, her bein' one and all."

"Andy'll take good care of Barbara," Sheriff Rodriguez said confidently, "But it's still not like being with family."

"J.T., I ain't been part of the family since Barbara's daddy kicked me outta the hospital room the night Miriam died." His face reddened, and the pale blue eyes turned cold. He deftly dodged the cow's hooves as she scrambled to her feet, wiped his sweating face with an old blue bandana and walked out of the barn and into the morning sunshine.

"You ought to at least go see Barbara," the sheriff called after him.

Gabriel kept walking. He was tired of arguing and besides, he never did like people telling him what he should do and shouldn't do. Grady was waiting for him beside the old truck.

"What are we gonna owe you, Gabe?" the foreman asked.

"I'll just add it to your bill, if I can find it."

Gabriel leaned over the hood of his pickup, squinting

48

in the sunlight, running a crooked forefinger over the numbers that had been scribbled on the paint with a pencil. Gabriel never carried a pad with him. When he finished a job, he simply did his figuring on the truck. He said it reminded folks to pay him every time they saw him driving down the road.

"Let's see," the old man said to himself, scanning the hood. "This one was the twin calves over at Albert's. And here's the sick goat at Garcia's. The pig with the colic at George's."

Gabriel suddenly licked his thumb and wiped out that set of figures.

"The pig died," he said. "George called me too late."

He paused, and his hand followed the row of numbers until he reached a column just to the right of the left headlight. "Here you are, Grady," Gabriel said. "Let's see, what'd we have today? Twenty-two cows at five bucks a head, plus mileage, minus the cornbread and sorghum you brought me for breakfast. I'll just put you down for an even hundred bucks."

"You sure that's enough?"

"Just see that Wilson pays me before we get a rain and it washes away the bill."

Grady grinned.

Gabriel opened the door of his truck. He never hung around any place for very long. He had miles to travel before the day ended, even if he didn't have anywhere in particular to go.

Sheriff Rodriguez grabbed his arm. "You just gonna walk out on the little girl and forget her?" He was mad now, not about to let the old man run from his responsibility.

"J.T., I was always pretty good with calves and yearlings. But I have as much business with a kid as I have with a sore-tempered rattlesnake."

For the first time, a smile spread across the sheriff's face. "You're scared of both of 'em, aren't you?"

Gabriel spit his cigar out onto the ground. "A rattlesnake wouldn't really bother me much," he answered while crawling into the old truck. "Shoot, I could throw it out in the cold if the doggone thing bit me."

He paused.

Then he added, "I don't have any idea in the world what you do with a little girl."

"You did once, Gabe."

Gabriel stared in silence, and he remembered, and he abruptly drove away trying to erase the memories that haunted him.

5

Rebel stood patiently beside the wooden corral fence, as motionless as a statue on the courthouse square, while Barbara dipped her sponge into a large tub of soapy water and began wiping a coat of caliche dust off the big sorrel's neck. It was a ritual that both girl and horse knew well. On the afternoon James Atkins first tied Rebel to the mesquite post behind his house, Barbara had taken an old, ragged towel and washed down the sorrel, talking to him, whispering to him, calming the wild eyes that darted nervously around new and strange surroundings. She hadn't missed a day since, save one, the day she gave up her father to the hard, sun-baked West Texas ground that he had always loved so much.

Rebel turned his head and playfully nuzzled Barbara. She laughed, pulling a licorice jelly bean from the pocket of her red-checked shirt and letting the horse take it from her hand. He snorted and nipped at her sleeve, looked for more, and Barbara threw her frail arms around his thick neck, hugging him tightly.

With Rebel, she could forget, or at least suspend, the anguish that simmered inside of her. With Rebel, the summers never seemed quite so hot or the winters nearly so cold. With him, the day was bright even if the sun forgot to shine. With Rebel, she never felt alone, not even now, when she no longer had anyone to go home to.

Barbara had always been able to sit for hours and talk to the big sorrel, and he always listened. Perhaps Rebel didn't understand, but he never ran away or laughed at her. He never ridiculed the row of freckles that were scattered like cockleburs across her nose.

Rebel's ears suddenly perked up, and Barbara could hear the sound of a car grinding its way across the field, through the weeds and toward the corral. She smiled and waved as Andy slid out of the Chevette and headed toward her.

"You're early," Barbara said.

"It doesn't take long to write a gardening column for the newspaper when there's no water to put on the flowers anyway." Andy had stuffed the legs of her jeans inside her boots, and Barbara thought it made her look more like a high fashion model out of Dallas than a cowgirl.

"So what did you say?"

"I just told 'em to drill a hole two inches deep, spit on the seed, drop it in the ground, then pray for rain." Andy paused, then shook her head. "I'm worried," she said. "I'm beginning to sound more like Gabriel every day."

At the mention of the old man's name, the smile faded from Barbara's face. Pain pricked her like a thorn and was reflected in her eyes, sometimes sad, sometimes bitter. She turned away without another word and again ran the sponge across Rebel's muscled back, his coat glistening burnt red in the glow of the afternoon sunlight.

Andy rolled up her sleeves, dug around in the tub until she found another sponge, and began washing the dust from his face, stopping only long enough to untangle a stray grassbur buried in his mane.

She stepped back, looking over her shoulder as Sheriff Rodriguez pulled his patrol car close beside hers. He eased out of the front seat and clamped his Stetson tightly on his head before the strong winds could whip it out of his hand.

"I went out to see Gabriel this morning," he said.

Andy lost her smile, too. She folded her arms in defiance. Her blonde ponytail lay limply on a shoulder, and her shirt hung loosely around a slender waist. Her jeans fit snugly, perhaps washed a few too many times.

Andy Beck had long presented an enigma to Caprock. A lot of young bull riders had a crush on her. The older bull riders wanted to court her. The wise old men swore she was married to her job, more determined to prove that a woman could do a man's work than she was in becoming a man's wife. Maybe they were right.

"So you went out to see Gabe Spencer," Andy said rhetorically. The tone of her voice was a brittle as shattered glass.

Sheriff Rodriguez nodded.

53

"What was he doing? Convincing somebody to soak pumpkin seeds in kerosene, then bury them to get rid of the jake leg?"

"I talked to him about Barbara." The Sheriff leaned against the hood of his car. "Whether you like it or not, Andy, he is her grandfather. And by all rights, I guess, he should be her guardian."

"He's an ornery old reprobate who's not fit to look after Barbara."

"He barks a lot," the Sheriff admitted. "And he barks a little too loud sometimes. But he hasn't bitten anybody to speak of. Not lately, anyway. When you cut through all that bull of his, old Gabe's as solid as a rock. Folks around here have been depending on him for years."

"I haven't." The words startled Andy and the Sheriff both. They looked around and saw Barbara standing between their shadows on the ground. There was a sadness in her face, and her voice had no life to it at all. Barbara had obviously overheard much of their conversation, and Andy felt embarrassed, angry at herself for being so careless. Barbara had suffered enough. She certainly didn't need anyone criticizing her only living relative behind her back.

"Gabe's got no use for me," the girl said flatly. "He never has."

Andy, her harsh judgment of the old man suddenly tempered, knelt and put her arm around Barbara to comfort her. "No, Barb," she said quietly. "Gabe's just a cranky old man who's lived by himself too long. He just doesn't understand young girls, that's all."

"Daddy said he always blamed my grandmother for dying and leaving him by himself. Then he blamed my mama for getting married and leaving her by himself again. Then she died, and he lost her for good. And he didn't want anybody else." She paused, and her lips trembled. "Especially me."

"Don't believe that, Barbara." Andy gently pulled the girl to her. She felt so small, so fragile, just a skinny-legged girl with scratches on her knees who had been left shrunken and hollow-eyed by the tragedy.

"My mama died the night I was born, and I think Gabe thought it was my fault that she wasn't still alive. The only time I ever saw her face was in a picture, and she was laughing. I never *heard* her laugh at all."

Barbara slowly walked away, her scuffed boots kicking up puffs of dust from the driveway, her shoulders sagging, her head bowed. Andy watched her for a moment, then looked up at the Sheriff.

"You still think Gabriel's best for her?" she asked.

Rodriguez didn't answer.

"Did he even say he wanted her?"

The Sheriff sighed and shook his head.

"Has he ever loved her?"

"Maybe." Rodriguez watched Barbara lead her big sorrel away. "Maybe not."

"Does he even care?"

"Only Gabriel knows what he feels." The sheriff opened the door to his patrol car and adjusted his Stetson. "I can't judge him, Andy. I've never walked a mile in his boots, and neither have you."

55

Andy's face reddened.

Rodriguez cleared his throat and continued, "All I know is Miss Hightower over at the Welfare Department wants Barbara to get moved into a permanent home as soon as possible."

"She's living with me," Andy replied matter-of-factly.

"Miss Hightower wants it all done legal and tied up with red tape. There'll be a court hearing at nine o'clock in the morning on who'll be given custody of Barbara. Judge Stout's court. I'd appreciate your seeing that the girl gets there on time."

Andy's eyes were cold, her jaw clenched, and her hands drawn into small fists. She wanted to hit someone or something, but she didn't know who or what. Barbara had suffered enough. Why wouldn't people leave her alone? Why was someone always trying to cause problems for her? Andy answered without emotion, "We'll be there."

That night, as she carried the supper dishes to the kitchen sink, Barbara asked, "What are they gonna do to me?" Her words were barely audible.

"It'll be all right, Barb," Andy tried to comfort her. "Don't worry." She prayed that Barbara believed her, but she doubted it. She certainly didn't believe herself.

"Are they gonna take me away from here?"

"I'm sure it's just a formality."

Barbara had felt anger, then self-pity, then a sense of loneliness. Now fear knotted her stomach, and it gnawed deeper, and it wouldn't go away. She ran to her room and sat in the darkness, afraid to confront the morning, uncertain of what it held for her, refusing to close her eyes, knowing that sleep would only make the night pass faster and bring the daylight quicker than she was ready for it to come.

Barbara tried to stay awake, but her eyes wouldn't cooperate. They kept closing and sleep came in short, fitful doses. In her dreams, she kept running across hot, open fields, chasing Rebel, unable to catch him. Sometimes she couldn't even see him and knew she would never see him again. She kept calling his name, begging him to come home again, not knowing where home really was.

The hillsides she ran were steep, the grassburs sharp, and she ran alone because there was no one to run with her. The sound of her own voice awoke Barbara with a start. For a minute she didn't know where she was, then she did, and she cried silently into a pillow that was already wet with perspiration.

The stone courthouse, since 1871, had been the architectural centerpiece of downtown Caprock. It was prairie gothic in style, a solemn, almost forbidding kind of place, and a row of handcarved gargoyles frowned from the tower upon the southern side of town.

For Barbara, the courthouse had always been a place to approach with a certain amount of apprehension. She had walked around it many times in her life, but had never wanted to enter those darkened doorways. Now she had no other choice.

Barbara paused beneath the limbs of the old hanging tree and stared upward at the ancient clock that loomed above her. Eight forty-five. The morning, she thought, had taken forever to find Caprock. Yet it had come much too quickly, and she wanted to reach out and stop the hands on the clock. But time, too, seemed to have turned its back on her.

Questions kept tumbling in her mind, and she had no answers to any of them. What would become of her? Would she stay with Andy, or would she be taken away by somebody else? Do courts really care about what happens to little girls? Does anyone? Why was her daddy dead? And her mama? Why couldn't she just shut her eyes and let all of this go away?

Barbara had known what it was like to be alone. But fear was new to her, and she was afraid and didn't really understand why. She was surrounded by friends. She could see them waiting on the courthouse steps for her. But they seemed so far away. And somehow their faces seemed so unfamiliar. Barbara felt as though she wanted to cry, but she couldn't. Not anymore.

She kept walking forward, each step filled with nervous apprehension. Feeling sorry for herself wouldn't help anymore, and she was simply too tired to run away.

Whatever happened, she knew her life would never be the same again.

Barbara was wearing her black dress, the only one she owned, and she hated the ruffles on its sleeves. She had argued in favor of denim jeans, but Andy had told her that no judge would give a girl any consideration if she ambled into his courtroom as though it were a rodeo arena. Barbara didn't want to admit it, but Andy was probably right. She usually was.

The girl's hair had been curled, and it dropped in ringlets on her shoulders. She didn't feel comfortable or at ease with herself at all. When Barbara had glanced in the big plate glass window of Murphy's Drugstore, she hadn't even recognized the little freckle-faced lady staring back at her. The reflection was a mockery of who and what she was.

Andy stood beside her in a cool beige suit, looking much more like a professional white-collar business woman than a county agent. She smiled, sighed nervously, and nodded at Sheriff Rodriguez who came strolling out from behind the thick oak doors.

"You waiting on us, Sheriff?" Andy asked.

"Not officially." He patted Barbara's shoulder. "How're you feeling this morning?"

"Okay." Her voice was not convincing.

"You look mighty pretty all dressed up that way," the sheriff said, trying to cheer her up.

"I only wear this dress when I'm losing somebody."

Barbara stared straight ahead, and Rodriguez remembered the last time he had seen it. She had worn it to the funeral, and he wished he had kept his mouth shut. Drunks didn't bother him. Neither did speeders and bootleggers on Saturday night. But it seemed like everytime he tried to talk to a woman of any age he wound up with his foot in his mouth. He sighed, and Andy took his arm.

"I'm glad you're here," she said.

He pushed the brim of his Stetson down lower over his eyes and answered, "I like to know what goes on in my neck of the woods."

"Even when it's bad?"

Sheriff Rodriguez shrugged, "In my business," he said,

"it usually is."

They heard Gabriel B. Spencer's pickup truck long before they saw it turn beside Wilson's National Bank building and cough its way down Main Street. Rocks had knocked the muffler off months before, the radiator was patched, and some swore the old man had figured out a way to run it on kerosene instead of gasoline. Gabriel spent about as much time driving across prairie as he did on road. He simply believed that the shortest distance between two points was a straight line, and sometimes the highway didn't run in a straight line.

Gabriel parked alongside the curb and yelled to the sheriff as he limped across the lawn. "I don't know why you wanted me up here this mornin', J.T."

"You're the girl's grandfather, Gabe."

"I didn't ask to be her grandfather." The grizzled old man bit a plug out of his cold cigar and spit it on the ground. "I didn't want Miriam marryin' that doggone seed salesman in the first place."

"Miss Hightower thought it'd be best if you showed up," the sheriff replied calmly. As far as he was concerned, the cantankerous old man was a lot like a rattlesnake with its venom gone. He would still bite you, but he no longer did any harm.

Gabriel stretched as though he had just crawled out of bed, looked up at the courthouse clock, then growled, "That old biddy just likes to throw her weight around, and she's got plenty of it to throw. Makes her feel important. She roots around people's lives like a hog in a mud hole. Don't get nothin' out of it but dirt up her nose."

61

He labored up the steps, pausing beside Barbara, and for a moment his eyes caught hers. He rubbed his beard and, in embarrassment the girl turned away. The silence was awkward, and neither knew quite what to say. Barbara was tense and nervous, almost as flustered as Gabriel. Above them, the clock chimed nine times.

"You sure are doin' a good job of growin' up," the old man said at last.

Barbara nodded timidly.

Gabriel grinned, and she thought that for a brief second she had seen a fleeting twinkle in his eyes. "Seems like I always think of you as bein' knee-high to a jackrabbit."

Barbara opened her mouth to speak, but no words came out and Gabriel looked away.

"But then," he muttered to himself, "I always remember your mama the same way."

He limped into the courthouse alone.

Judge Stout had a voice like thunder. He could quiet his courtroom with a single word. His hair was white, and his face looked as though it had been chiseled out of pure granite. He didn't need a black robe to give him dignity. He wasn't as wise as Solomon, perhaps, but he had just as much patience. He believed in arriving at the truth, no matter how long it took. There was justice in his voice and compassion in his eyes. He seated himself, leaned back in his chair, folded his hands beneath his chin, and looked out at the room.

Judge Stout saw Barbara first, her face pinched, barely breathing, quite uncomfortable and out of place in that black dress with ruffled sleeves. She should have worn jeans, he thought. Racing the barrels, Barbara had always appeared to be so confident, so formidable. Now she looked as pitiful as a lost puppy in a cold rain, with no place to keep warm, and that troubled the judge. He only hoped she would be happier when the morning ended. He didn't know if the letter of the law would allow it.

Beside Barbara sat Andy Beck, more of a big sister than a mother figure. Andy, for most of the girls in Caprock, had been a teacher, a role model, a friendly ear who listened to their problems and offered advice only when she was asked for it. The judge often wondered if Andy hadn't chosen the wrong profession. Most of what she knew about the land came from books, not from experience.

She was a city girl who had learned about horses at a riding academy, whose garden had been two rows of beans and a row of tomatoes plowed in the St. Augustine grass out in the backyard of her home. A drought had not yet seared her soul. The bawling of thirsty cattle had not yet kept her awake at night.

She had never watched farmers trying to grow crops when the wind kept blowing away the topsoil. She had never seen cattle turn their backs to a blue norther blizzard and lay down to die in the snow.

But she would. And could she handle it when it happened? Would she run away and head back to the warm neon shelter of the city? If she did, what would happen to Barbara?

Behind them huddled a few friends who had come to

show their interest in the girl. Ricky was idly scratching his face with the feather on his bullrider's hat, as uneasy as he had always been in a church pew on Sunday morning. Mrs. Turner sat holding Kathy's hand. The Madrones had their heads bowed. Perhaps they were praying. Judge Stout hoped they remembered his name, but not in vain.

Arnold Edwards had closed his store and slipped in to sit alongside Gabriel. Arnold could always be depended on to pay his respects when they were needed. Gabriel's chin had dropped to his chest. His eyes were closed. To all the world, he looked like he was asleep, but the judge knew better. He had played too many hands of dominoes with the old man. Gabriel had an uncanny knack of looking disinterested even when he wasn't.

He was dangerous that way — his face was like the double blank. He had a habit of winning, even when he looked like a beaten man. Gabriel had a habit of winning, even when he didn't draw good dominoes, which was seldom. The judge never knew what to expect from Gabriel B. Spencer. But the judge never counted him out.

Down front, Miss Hightower was busily shuffling through the papers in her leather briefcase, whispering to her attorney. Her thin silver-rimmed glasses set perched near the end of her nose, held around her neck by a chain. There were streaks of silver sprinkled in her dark hair, pulled back into a bun on the back of her head.

It was obvious that Miss Hightower was the kind of dedicated state employee who was strictly business. She had a job to do, and she knew how to do it well. She never cared how she finished in a popularity contest, which was usually near the bottom. She was wearing a gray suit and white blouse, nothing frilly, nothing feminine. Miss Hightower stacked the papers neatly beside her briefcase and glanced over the rim of her glasses at Barbara, her thin lips pinched into a perpetual frown.

Judge Stout couldn't remember ever having heard her laugh, and he wondered sometimes if she had ever been a child at all. Miss Hightower simply brought her attorney along because it seemed like the proper thing to do. She seldom let him speak and never let him think out loud. To her, he was just one of the legal tools it took to nail down a righteous and judicious decision, about as easily overlooked as the fine print on the last page of a document that nobody ever read.

Judge Stout slipped his horn-rim glasses back on, quickly scanned the legal brief that had been placed before him, then leaned forward and smiled at Barbara, hoping to reassure her that anything he said would be strictly in her best interest. He had no bones to pick with anyone. He simply wanted to find a good home for the little girl and to get out of town while the catfish were still biting down in the Rio Grande.

The judge cleared his throat and drawled, "Well, as you know we're here this morning to determine the permanent custody of a minor child, Miss Barbara Gail Atkins, whose mother and father are both deceased. Under the emergency protection articles of the state family code, she has been staying with Miss Andy Beck until the court appoints a managing conservator."

He paused and his gaze narrowed in the direction of Gabriel, whose battered hat was removed from his balding head and laid respectfully in his lap. "I believe Miss Atkins has only one living relative —" the judge continued, "a grandfather — one Gabriel B. Spencer. Is that right?"

Judge Stout waited for an answer.

Gabriel didn't bother to even open his eyes. He sat mute, like an aging statue that had been dragged in out of the rain.

Andy glanced at Barbara and realized that the young girl was petrified, trembling, unable to speak, not even knowing what she was supposed to say, if anything.

Andy spoke for her. "Yes, your honor. That's right."

The judge frowned, leaned back informally, took off his glasses again, and rubbed his eyes. "Gabe, come here," he said with resignation. "I need to talk to you about what to do with this little girl."

The old man grunted and rose slowly to his feet, taking the cigar plug he had been chewing and dropping it in a brass cuspidor beside the benches. Clutching his hat with both hands, he ambled down the aisle, cocking his head to one side and squinting at the judge as though an old fishing partner had just become an adversary.

"Roy," he said, "you want me to just stand here or get up there in that witness stand of yours?"

"Wherever's the most comfortable."

Gabriel nodded and stood slightly bowed before the bench.

"How old are you, Gabe?" the judge asked as kindly

66

and quietly as he could.

"I was sixty-three last month, Roy."

"You ready to take on the responsibility of raising this little girl?"

Gabriel snorted like a wild mustang that had just been led into a corral where he didn't belong. He looked around at Barbara, then back toward the judge.

"I ain't hardly got the time, Roy," he said, hitching up his pants. "My pole beans are dyin', an' I knocked a hole in my muffler goin' out to check on Albert's twin calves, an' the termites done ate up my fence posts, an'. . ."

Gabriel paused, glanced at Barbara again and took a deep, painful breath. "Shoot, Roy," he admitted, "I'm just too old and set in my ways to start over again."

"Then, as grandfather and the only living relative of Barbara Gail Atkins, you waive your rights to the girl." The judge frowned and his voice was harsh.

Gabriel didn't notice. He nodded, smiled broadly and answered loudly, "I think she'll do just fine with Miss Andy there. They're like two peas in a pod anyhow."

"Thank you, Gabe." The judge turned his attention again to the legal brief. "You can sit down now."

The old man eased into a seat behind Barbara, reached over and patted her shoulder. He leaned back and closed his eyes and hoped that Judge Stout would go ahead and make up his mind before he wasted the whole morning.

"Miss Hightower," the judge said crisply, "is the Department of Public Welfare agreeable to Barbara being placed under the permanent care of Miss Andy Beck?"

67

Barbara held her breath.

Andy took her hand and grasped it tightly.

Miss Hightower rose to her feet, formal and erect. She was now in charge, and that was the place she liked to be. She spoke, and the words snapped off her tongue like the crack of a whip.

"Your Honor," she said, "that type of situation is not exactly what our guidelines call for. This, of course, is no reflection on Miss Beck. She is a respected and appreciated member of our community. But we feel that we must ask that Barbara Atkins be placed in a true family atmosphere."

The little girl gasped. Her heart had already been broken. Now it was shattered.

Barbara, her eyes wide, looked up at Andy and saw only confusion and bewilderment in the face of her friend. Andy rose to speak, but Miss Hightower cut her off.

"Miss Beck is a single woman," she said sharply, "and in our studies, in our investigations, we have always found that that kind of chaotic environment can be permanently detrimental to the well-being of a minor female. It's best for the girl if she has the loving, religious guidance of both a mother and a father. Your Honor, I have a list of foster homes we have already investigated and approved." Her smile was devoid of all humor.

"Is one available?" the judge asked.

"Yes, your Honor. We have a couple waiting right now in Houston."

Barbara sat is disbelief. She was being uprooted and

moved away, and there was nothing she could do about it. And nobody had even asked her where she wanted to live. Nobody cared.

She was a minor, they said. And that gave everybody the right to make up her mind for her. Barbara wanted to run. She had to get away. But where could she go? Where could she hide? And what about Rebel? She bet they didn't even allow horses in Houston.

Andy had eased out into the aisle and now took a step toward the judge. Her eyes were pleading. "Houston is five hundred miles away," she argued. "All of Barbara's friends are right here in Caprock."

"She'll make new ones," Miss Hightower snapped.

Barbara's shoulders slumped, and a tear wet the freckles on her cheek.

Behind her, Gabriel opened one eye, then the other. He heard the quiet sobs of a young girl, and he saw the smile on Miss Hightower's face. It was a little too haughty to suit him. He suddenly slapped the back of the wooden bench with his hat and raised his voice in disgust, "Roy, are you gonna let that old biddy get away with that?"

Judge Stout shrugged and pitched the legal brief aside. "I'm afraid I'll have too, Gabe. You've left me no choice."

Gabriel placed a strong hand on Barbara's shoulder and asked, "What's gonna happen to her?"

"She'll be placed in a good foster home," the judge told him. "And maybe even adopted out."

"To strangers?"

"That's the way it usually is."

"Houston's a big city," Gabriel said bluntly. "Ain't

69

nobody got any business in a big city."

"There's a couple of million people who'll disagree with you." Judge Stout grinned and folded his arms.

Gabriel shoved an unlit cigar back in his mouth, and said, "Out in the country, you can breathe if the sand ain't blowin' too much. You got room to stand tall and room to grow without crowdin' anybody. You got coyotes to sing you to sleep at night and a good, strong wind to push you on if you ever think of givin' up, and folks who'll do you a favor even if they don't know you.

"You learn to appreciate the rain 'cause we hardly ever have any of it. You learn to forgive a rainbow for lyin' to you and appreciate it because it's just so doggone pretty. You can watch a stubborn old mesquite tree and learn that nobody can whip you even if you don't amount to nothin'. Out here in the country, everybody is somebody, and a man's handshake is more bindin' than one of them legal contracts a two-bit lawyer draws up in self-defense.

"You can't say that about a city, any of 'em. The only good thing you can say about a city is that it keeps all of them people from comin' out here."

Gabriel paused, wiped a smattering of loose tobacco leaves off his lips and looked up at the judge. "You ever want to live in the city, Roy?"

"Can't say as I ever did."

Gabriel looked down at Barbara and said softly, "Well, maybe she don't either."

"I'm sorry, Gabe," the judge answered. "I'm all out of options. Miss Hightower knows the law. She follows the law, and what she's suggested is about the only thing we have left to do."

Gabriel thrust his hands in his back pockets and rocked back in defiance. "I'm still her grandfather, ain't I?"

"That you are."

"Then by law, Barbara belongs to me."

The judge shook his head. "You waived your rights to her, Gabe."

"Well, doggone it, Roy," the old man yelled, "I'm waivin' 'em back."

Miss Hightower twirled on her high heels and faced Gabriel, her smile gone, her eyes glowering at him. "And what does an old man like you know about the welfare of a little girl?" she said, hammering out each word.

"That she's a lot better off here than there," Gabriel countered, "wherever there happens to be."

Miss Hightower slammed her briefcase shut and glared at Judge Stout. "You're not going to let him get away with this, are you?"

The flicker of a smile crept into the corners of the judge's mouth. "Well," he answered slowly, "if Gabe is willin' to give it a shot, I certainly am."

"He's nothing but a troublemaker."

"He's blood kin."

"Sometimes that's not enough." Miss Hightower removed her glasses, turned to face Gabriel and warned, "I'll be keeping an eye on you, Mr. Spencer. If you ever give me a reason to prove you're not fit, I'll take that girl away from you so fast Judge Stout won't have time to even bang his gavel."

"Honey," Gabriel said sweetly, "you're just lucky the

Good Lord didn't reel you in, take a good look, and throw you back."

Barbara walked out into the harsh sunlight, not really sure if she had won or lost. Caprock would still be home. Rebel would be close, and so would friends like Ricky, Lisa, and Kathy. Their mothers all hugged her neck and told her they were glad she was staying. Mrs. Madrone had been crying. Andy seemed relieved. The sheriff kept shaking everyone's hand and talking about how he loved to see justice work out right for a change.

Gabriel was another story. He was her grandfather, yet she didn't know him and probably never would. Now she would be living under the same roof with him, and she wondered if he was as rough as his voice could be.

"What are you gonna do now?" Andy asked as Gabriel paused on the top step of the courthouse.

The old man scratched his head and his eyes met those of Barbara. They looked to him like those of a cottontail rabbit caught in barbwire with a coyote on its tail.

"You got me," he said. "I guess I finally have somebody to talk to. But I'm not too sure it ever talks back."

Barbara glanced away. She had nothing to say.

"Let's go, girl," Gabriel told her, "we've wasted enough time already, and there's a good twelve hours of sunshine still waitin' on us out there."

He walked on down the steps, but Barbara was reluctant to follow. She reached for Andy, needing support, needing someone to reassure her, feeling foolish, alone and afraid.

Gabriel stopped beneath the low-hanging limbs of the

hanging tree and motioned her to hurry along. "Come on, girl. Or the cow's gonna curdle 'fore you get her milked."

Barbara felt Andy nudge her gently and whisper, "It's okay, Barb. I'll be close if you need me."

"I'm scared."

"Don't worry," Andy said and smiled, "so is he."

With hesitation in her steps, Barbara slowly trailed after the old man who was already sauntering off across the courthouse lawn. She had hoped that Gabriel would wait for her, but somehow was glad he hadn't. Too many years had passed since she had last seen him climbing into that old pickup of his to drive slowly away, leaving her, forgetting her, she sometimes thought, for good. Barbara had often wondered what it would be like to have a grandfather who laughed with her, sang with her, told her stories when it was time for bed at night.

She never knew. Her heart ached, and there was a knot in her stomach. Was it because she didn't want to be with Gabriel? Or was it because she was afraid he didn't want her around? The old man slammed the door of his truck and honked the horn. And Barbara found herself running at last toward him.

Standing on the steps, Andy sighed as Rodriguez walked to her side. "I don't know whether to thank the old reprobate or curse him," she said. "It just worries me. I didn't want to lose Barbara. Gabriel's just too uncivilized to take care of her."

"There are lots of folk around here who'd disagree with you, Andy. Gabe's been doing their horse doctorin' for them a long time now."

73

"Yeah," Andy sighed. "And he doesn't even have a license."

"You don't need one for raising a kid," the sheriff replied as he watched Gabriel's pickup truck chug down the street, run one red light, turn beside Arnold's Feed Store and head for the far side of town. He could hear the engine coughing and complaining long after he had lost sight of the truck.

The house on the corner had once been painted white, but the years and the sandstorms had left it a dingy gray, scarred and splintered, a derelict on the wrong side of town. The roof sagged, and several of the shingles had been pried loose by a north wind and tossed carelessly into the backyard. The red trim had faded and was peeling. A good many of the boards on the front porch obviously needed to be replaced.

Gabriel, hands on his hips, scowled as he stood on the cracked cement sidewalk watching Barbara drag a tattered cardboard suitcase out the front door.

"It sure don't look like much," he said of the house. "I'm just glad Miriam never had to live in this dump."

"It was a good home," Barbara answered defiantly.

"How many did you have, anyway, child? Seven? Eight?" Gabriel took the suitcase from her and pitched it into the back of his truck. "Seems like every time your daddy got a couple of months behind on his rent, ya'll was up an' movin' again."

"Daddy was always looking for something better."

"He sure as heck didn't find it."

"He would have."

Gabriel snorted with disgust and ambled up the sidewalk. "Honey," he said, "rainbows didn't follow your daddy's side of the family. Only rain."

"Daddy worked hard."

"But he never made enough money to put gravy on his meat."

Barbara's eyes were seared with pain, and resentment cut through her. She clenched her fists until the knuckles turned white, staring at the old man who, Barbara decided, didn't really care if she lived or she died. He had taken her only to save face in front of his friends. He didn't want her. But then he never had.

And there was a bitterness buried deep inside of Gabriel, a discontent that he had put away years ago. Now he felt it boiling up inside of him. "That was your daddy's problem, girl," he said. "He didn't know what he had. He didn't know what he wanted. And he didn't have enough gumption to go after it."

"My daddy loved me," Barbara said, her words as cold as a blue norther.

"What'd he ever do for you."

"He always got home in time to watch me and Rebel run. He took me swimming and he read me stories. One time, when my kitten ran away, he stayed up all night till he found her." Barbara's tears of remorse had turned to anger. "He tucked me in bed every night, and when I hurt my hand he'd kiss it and make it better, and if we only had one chicken leg left he'd give it to me. And that's better'n money any stinkin' day."

She broke and ran into the dark interior of the house as Gabriel yelled, "And what did he leave you?"

Barbara didn't answer.

"Nothin'," the old man said gruffly. "But then, you never had anything to begin with, just two-bit junk and a rent house. Don't do you any good. Pay that money every month to a landlord and when you die they take it away from you and you ain't got nothin'."

Gabriel stepped inside the living room, lit only by a narrow sliver of sunlight that crept past the broken venetian blinds. The walls were bare, save the one dime-store plaque that said, *THERE'S NO PLACE LIKE HOME.* An old hand-me-down quilt had been thrown over the sofa to hide the holes, and an overstuffed chair had been patched so many times it reminded Gabriel of the inner tubes on his old Model T jalopy back when roads were nothing more than a pair of well-worn ruts in the prairie.

"You know what your daddy should have done with his money?" Gabriel asked loudly.

There was no answer.

"He should've bought land with it." The old man gingerly removed the wall plaque and tossed it onto the sofa. "A man who's got land," he continued, "owns the whole world — or at least a damn good piece of it."

Barbara knew she was standing in her bedroom for the

last time. It had once been her refuge, a place to hide and dream and be alone. A place to run barrel races in her mind, races she never lost. A place where she had whispered her hopes, plans, fears, and the secrets no one else would ever know. It had seemed so warm, then. So intimate. So much a part of her. Now it, too, was being taken from her. She would never again lie on her bed and watch the flowers in her wallpaper bloom in spring.

Slowly she began removing the barrel racing ribbons from the wall, packing them alongside her trophies in a cardboard box, pausing a moment to relive the memory of each. Her first race. The first race she won. The night she fell. The night the last barrel fell. The night the record fell. All were important to her. Maybe Gabriel had been right. She hadn't had much in life. But she had been a winner, and nobody could ever take that away from her.

In the dining room behind her, Barbara could hear the old man stumbling through the dimly-lit room, shoving the plastic furniture out of his way and mumbling, "There ain't nothin' better than a chunk of dirt with your name written on it. A man's home is his castle and land makes you a king. James wasn't smart enough to know that. Land makes you amount to something. A little land would've given that girl a real good stake to get started with."

Gabriel stopped in the doorway of Barbara's bedroom and said with finality, "Now all she's got is what he left her with. Nothin'."

Barbara rummaged through the trunk and found the framed picture. She looked carefully at the eight-by-ten black and white photograph, which was a little grainy and almost out of focus. Rebel was standing proud, his head held high. And she was on his back clutching the championship trophy. Holding the big sorrel's reins was her daddy. He was smiling happily, and he was smiling right at her.

Time hadn't changed that. Time never would. That smile, that day would belong to her forever. Barbara grinned back, and a tear stained her cheek. For a moment, she hugged the photograph to her chest, then placed it carefully among the trophies. She then grabbed the cardboard box and ran out of the room, almost bumping into Gabriel as she bolted without a word into the hallway.

Outside, Barbara didn't stop until she reached the corral at the far end of a dirt pathway that led toward a small, rusting, makeshift tin barn. Rebel whinnied as he saw her dashing across the field, standing with his head stretched out above the wooden fence, nonchalantly switching flies with his tail. Barbara gently laid the box in the short, brown, sun-charred grass and scrambled to the top rung of the corral, grabbing Rebel's thick neck and burying her face in his mane, which was the color of wheat. Her frail body shook with the grief and hurt inside her. Rebel patiently waited for the licorice jelly beans Barbara always carried with her.

On the front porch of the rent house, Gabriel watched the girl cling to her horse and sadly shook his head. Barbara had been with him for less than an hour and already she had defied him twice, ignored him every chance she got, sassed him once, and spent the rest of the time crying. Maybe she would have been better off in Houston among strangers after all, he told himself. They certainly couldn't have made any bigger mess of things than he had.

He didn't know what to say to the girl, so figured everything he said was wrong. He didn't know what she liked or didn't like, other than the fact she didn't care much for him, and he didn't really blame her.

Dang it! He had told J.T. and the judge both that he didn't have any business with a skinny-legged kid hanging around in his shadow. But they wouldn't listen to him. They had tricked him. They had bet on him being too dang ornery to put up with any of Miss Hightower's high-falutin' foolishness. And they had been right.

He would have been better off sitting on a creekbank than in a courtroom. He knew how to outsmart a catfish. But a smart-aleck judge had whipped him and whipped him good. Gabriel felt about like a poker player who had been betting on an ace when it was resting in somebody else's hand.

As he dragged the patched, overstuffed chair to the pickup truck, Gabriel was met by a middle-aged woman with a middle-aged smile, holding a dish that had been wrapped with a towel. Her hair was long and ratted onto the top of her head. She was wearing a feed-sack dress and a bright red-checked cotton apron. The lady tilted her head and introduced herself. "I'm Mrs. Simpson."

"Howdy ma'am."

"I thought the girl might need a little food for supper."

She handed Gabriel the bowl. It was so hot, he almost dropped it. He shoved it under one arm and blew on his scorched fingers to cool them.

"Son of a bearded buffalo!" he yelled. "What's in the bowl."

"Beans."

"What kind?"

"Red beans." Mrs. Simpson wiped her hands daintily on her apron. "I got 'em right out of the garden."

Gabriel carefully opened the lid and smelled. The steam hit him flush in the face. "Got any onions in them?"

"No."

"Any jalapeno peppers?"

"No."

"Any hot sauce or chili powder?"

"No."

Gabriel frowned and glanced out toward the corral. "Did you cook these for us?" he asked suspiciously, "or for the horse."

The lady, knowing an insult when she heard one, turned and walked away in a huff. "Just tell Barbara that they're from Mrs. Simpson down the road," she said, trying to be polite but aggravated with the old man.

Gabriel dipped one finger into the beans, licked the juice, and rolled his eyes in disbelief. "I've tasted rainwater with more seasonin' than this," he mumbled.

Mrs. Simpson didn't hear him.

He made sure of that. His whole life, he had always made it a rule to never fight with a mule, a wildcat, or a woman. A mule was too stubborn. A wildcat was too mean. And as far as Gabriel was concerned, a woman was worse than both of them. Now he had one living with him; a miniature perhaps, but she dressed like a female, acted like a female and talked like a female. He figured she no doubt fought like one, too.

He sighed and shuffled on down the dirt pathway toward the corral, lost in his own thoughts, his shoulders slumped as though he was carrying the weight of the whole world on his back, and she probably only balanced the scales at sixty pounds, boots and all.

Barbara had climbed to the top of the cedar post fence and was feeding licorice jelly beans to a calm and contented horse. The wind had dried her eyes and only a slight trace of dust adhered to the wetness that still lay upon her cheeks. She heard the old man coming but refused to look his way or acknowledge his presence.

Gabriel leaned his tired body against the corral fence and pushed his hat back further on his head. A cool silence had built a strong wall between him and the girl, and he was at a loss to know how to break it down.

Barbara nervously bit at her lip and stroked Rebel's mane, hoping the irritation would go away but knowing that it wouldn't as long as Gabriel was in the neighborhood.

Gabriel chewed on his cigar, even thought about lighting it but doubted if the hootchi-kootchie dancer painted on his cigarette lighter had enough fluid in her to keep a flame burning long enough. Instead, he held the bowl of steaming beans out to the horse and removed the fogged lid. Rebel sniffed them, then snorted. His nose twitched and he angrily shook his head, backing away from the fence and pawing uneasily at the earth.

Gabriel reached for a smile and found one. "Smart horse you got there," he said.

"Daddy bought him for me." Barbara's jaws were clenched tight. "And daddy trained him for me."

"He's big enough."

Barbara's voice softened. "Maybe jelly beans are good for him."

"Looks to me like he's got all the makin' of a pretty good work horse. Big. Strong. Got muscles in all the right places."

"Rebel was built to run."

Gabriel nodded. "They're all built to run," he said. "Some are just faster than others, that's all."

"None of 'em are faster than Rebel." It wasn't an argument, just a statement of fact.

"I'd rather have a goat." Gabriel bent over and shoved his right britches leg back into his boot. "Goats get fat eatin' tin cans that somebody else has paid for."

Barbara stiffened.

A cold hardness worked its way back into her eyes.

Gabriel realized he had upset her again. He silently cursed himself for being as gentle as a stray fox in a hen house and usually about as destructive. He had a serious problem with his mouth, he told himself. He never knew when or for how long to keep it shut. Gabriel patted the big sorrel's forehead, hoped his grin looked sincere, and said matter-of-factly, "But at least old Rebel's got enough sense to stay away from a bowl of washed-out beans."

"I can cook beans."

Gabriel looked at Barbara in surprise. "What kind of beans?" he asked.

" 'Most any kind."

Barbara paused, then added, "But daddy said I always cooked 'em hot enough to leave blisters on his tongue."

"Was the fire too hot?"

"Sometimes."

"And the peppers?"

"They were always hot."

The old man brightened and his eyes danced as though he had just found a four-leaf clover in a field of thistles. "Well, Barbara," he said softly, "we just may get along all right after all."

Gabriel took the girl's hand, holding it steady as she leaped to the ground. He pitched the beans into a stand of dry weeds, figuring they needed the water, stuck the empty bowl under his arm, and walked slowly with Barbara back toward the dingy white house with the sagging roof.

"When can we take Rebel out to your place?" Barbara asked timidly.

"When we got time, girl. Even God didn't get around to doin' everything in one day. It took him seven, and he was a lot younger than I am."

"Rebel misses me."

"Horses have a lot of sense sometime."

Gabriel had reached the old pickup truck before he realized that Barbara had not removed her hand from his. He felt the tight grip of her small, slender fingers. It was the oddest feeling he had experienced in a long time. Miriam had held his hand that way. But Miriam loved him. She wasn't a stranger. She wasn't an interloper in his life. Miriam had belonged.

The Caprock city limit sign read: POP. 7,341. But it had been peppered with slugs from somebody's single-shot twenty-two rifle, and Gabriel knew the figures were wrong anyway. Caprock, through the years, had finally gotten about as big as it was going to get, then it began to shrink. For the last decade, there had been no new buildings, no new businesses, no new faces or new blood. Kids grew up and moved away, and nobody ever came back down that long straight shot of a highway to replace them. Newcomers were even more rare than rain, but Caprock hung on and was held together simply by those who were to stubborn to ever turn their back on the land that had turned its back on them.

Gabriel drove his old pickup out onto the pavement, put Caprock in his rearview mirror, and wound his way slowly back into the hills. The sun had slipped into the late afternoon part of the sky and glared at him through the windshield. The old man didn't seem to mind. The windows were open, the winds were whistling through the truck, and Gabriel was humming an old gospel tune, pausing just long enough, now and then, to spit his well-seasoned tobacco juice out across the countryside.

Barbara had laid her head back on the frayed seat, staring beyond the brakes but oblivious to the world around her. Her arm was resting on Gabriel's black leather bag. She bounced each time the pickup hit a chuckhole, and Gabriel wasn't missing many of them.

"How old are you now, Barbara?" Gabriel asked, his words intruding past the wall of silence that the girl had built around her.

"Thirteen and a half."

"I had a thirteen-year-old horse once."

Gabriel paused.

"He snored," the old man said.

"Rebel doesn't snore."

"I know." Gabriel grinned. "All he does is run."

"Rebel is the fastest barrel horse there is in West Texas." Her face brightened, and the freckles seemed to fade when she smiled. "And when I'm ridin' him, I feel like I own the whole world."

Gabriel spit again and rubbed his mouth, wiping away the loose tobacco leaves. "You can't trust the world," he said. "It'll doublecross you every time. I know."

He glanced over at Barbara and whispered, "I owned the whole world once."

"What happened?"

"I lost it."

"How?"

"Tryin' to draw to an inside straight at a poker table I'd never sat at before, in a town I'd never been to."

Barbara straightened up and propped herself against the door. "What card did you need to win?" she asked.

"A deuce, a four, and a six."

She giggled.

Gabriel grinned.

And the tension between them began to thaw as surely

as spring weakens the grip winter always holds on the plains. For awhile they rode without speaking, at ease with themselves for a change, and comfortable with each other's company. Telephone poles, strung together with sagging wires, slipped with a static regularity outside the pickup's window. The juniper trees all leaned the same way, bent and twisted by the winds that sweep across the prairie without mercy and without ceasing. A jackrabbit, with long awkward legs and ears that seemed to drag in the dust, tried to outrun the truck and did. Overhead, a vulture with outspread wings caught another thermal current and sailed like a black kite in the sky, slowly circling, ever watchful for food that might be lying lifeless beside the highway.

Gabriel settled back, stroked his beard, and asked, "How long you reckon it's been since you seen my place?" He rolled the cold cigar from one corner of his mouth to the other.

"I was three years old when daddy took me to see you."

"He never brought you back," Gabriel retorted gruffly.

"You never asked me to come back." It was an accusation, an indictment that had been burning inside Barbara for a long time.

Gabriel didn't like the feeling of guilt that had reached out and touched him. He probably wasn't blameless. He hardly ever was. Some folks had even hinted that when the snake brought sin into the Garden of Eden, it was Gabriel who had turned the reptile loose. Just the same, he had never liked feeling guilty, even when he was. That was kind of like getting caught sneaking out of the hen house with eggs stuck in your pockets.

So he ignored her remark the best he could, and replied with the enthusiasm of a rainmaker who was trying to peddle clouds to a rancher whose land had been sucked dry and whose grasses were shriveling beneath his boots.

"The place has changed a lot, child," he said. "Back when you saw it last, all I had was a few stumps, a rusty barbed wire fence — an' that was down. There was a patch of yellow marigolds all bloomin' inside an old John Deere tractor tire out by the mailbox. Of course, that was before I fixed it up and poured the foundation for my sixteen-room house."

Gabriel beamed.

"It's got a view you won't believe," he bragged. "The only thing it ever needs to be the prettiest spot on this earth of ours is daylight."

Gabriel shut his eyes for a moment.

It didn't matter.

He had driven the road for so long he thought he owned it. He knew every bend in the highway and every crack in the pavement.

"Let me tell you," the old man said with a wink, "a little hard work has done wonders for the place. Barbara, you won't even recognize it."

Gabriel whipped the truck off the main road and bounced through a big rock gate, trimmed with wrought iron grillwork and hung with a newly-painted sign that said,

THREE EIGHT ESTATES
GABRIEL B. SPENCER, PROP.

88

The road became nothing more than a pair of worn-out ruts tracking back into the juniper and prickly pear. Barbara was hanging out the window, her eyes wide, obviously impressed with the pretentious gate. To her it looked more like the entryway to a mansion or, maybe, a cemetery.

"Well, this is it," Gabriel announced. "Look around you, honey, everything you see is mine."

"Everything?"

"Well, everything up close."

"Why did you name it Three Eight Estates?" Barbara brushed through her hair with her fingers and straightened her dress.

"'Cause I won the down payment one night in a Wichita Falls poker game."

"Holding three eights?"

Gabriel bit off the chewed end of his cigar and grinned. "The guy sittin' at the other side of the table sure thought I was."

"He quit?"

"No guts."

Barbara's face brightened. "*Did* you have three eights?" she asked.

Gabriel shrugged and replied softly, "Honey, in poker, you got to pay your money to see the cards."

He braked to a sudden stop, and Barbara whirled around quickly in her seat, taking in the whole landscape with one eager glance. Her face mirrored the shock and amazement that swept through her. Gabriel had been right. She didn't believe what she saw.

89

"Well, Barbara," the old man added, "this is home. There just ain't no place quite like it in the world."

Gabriel turned the key off in the ignition, and the pickup's tired engine coughed once, backfired, and died in the midst of its sputtering and its grumbling.

High weeds and thick vines had virtually overtaken a rusty mobile home that had been jammed rather crudely back into a cut in the hillside. All reminders that the trailer was once blue had been peeled away, save a strip along the south end that had been protected from the winds and rain by a post oak tree.

The front door step was simply an apple crate.

A television antenna lay in the yard, bent and disjointed, its wires torn loose and left to the mercy of the elements. Nearby, the concrete foundation for a house had been swallowed up by the underbrush. The few two-by-four partitions that had been left standing for walls hovered above the cement like rotting skeletons. Two rolls of barbwire were stacked on the foundation. The tin roof on a shack down beside the creek had fallen. A 1952 Studebaker was setting up on blocks, its windows broken and its motor missing. Half a dozen sun-blistered cornstalks rose up out of a garden that had lost out to the heat and the weeds.

Barbara tried to crawl out of the pickup, but her legs were weak. She blinked and looked around her again. "It looks like a ghost town," she muttered.

Gabriel shrugged. "Well, it might need a little touchin' up here and there," he confessed.

"But ghosts would be ashamed to live here." Barbara turned and faced the old man with bitterness edging into her voice. "So this is what a chunk of dirt looks like when it has your name written on it," she spit out. "If a man's home is really his castle, like you told me, then you're not much of a king."

Gabriel scowled. He didn't like to be cut down, especially with his own words.

"A splash of paint will fix it up all right," he argued. "An' the fence'll be as good as new soon as the rain washes the rust off."

"It never rains."

"Well, we're one day closer to rain than we've ever been before." Gabriel opened the door and pushed himself stiffly out of the truck.

"I thought you said you had a sixteen-room house," Barbara said loudly, following him out the door.

"I said I had the foundation for one." The old man stomped his way through the underbrush and stepped up on a broad slab of concrete, kicking a tin can out of his way. He took three steps, turned, and snapped, "All the house really needs is a few more walls, a closet or two, and a roof. Why, I'm standin' in the bedroom right now."

"It's falling down." Barbara crossed her arms and sat down with disgust on the running board of the old truck.

"The trailer isn't."

"Maybe not," Barbara agreed, then asked slowly, "but does it have a bathroom in it?"

Gabriel looked away, flustered and blushing with discomfort. He rubbed his face as her words sliced through him like the dull edge of a broken knife.

"Mostly, I just take a shovel and go to the pasture," he mumbled, ill at ease and somewhat embarrassed. Little girls could ask the dangdest questions, he thought. Why didn't she just go inside and look for a bathroom herself without bringing him into it. There were some things that men and women just didn't talk to each other about in public, and bathrooms was one of them. Barbara had the old man backed into a corner, and he decided to talk himself out of it. Gabriel limped toward the rolls of barbwire, picked up a dented bucket, and pitched it toward the girl.

"At least we got runnin' water," he yelled, then grinned slyly. "So why don't you run on down to the creek and get us some of it to wash up with before dinner."

Barbara, flabbergasted, shook her head, got up and walked toward the bucket, almost tripping over an antenna wire that was blocking her path.

"Your antenna's down," she called to Gabriel.

"Don't make no difference," Gabriel replied. "I ain't got no television."

"Why not?"

93

"I ain't got no electricity."

Barbara kicked the wire out of her way. "What's the matter?" she asked haughtily, "you didn't pay your bill?"

"That electricity fella came out one Friday and forgot and left my gate open," Gabriel answered defensively. "My cow got out, so I pulled the plug on 'em."

"That's not so smart."

"I don't need no electricity." Gabriel's voice suddenly sounded weary, cracked with age. "I go to bed when it gets dark."

"Just like the chickens?"

"I ain't got no chickens."

Gabriel pulled the tailgate down on the back of his pickup and, breathing heavily, slowly began to unload the bit and pieces of Barbara's furniture that she had insisted on bringing. Behind him, Barbara took the bucket and ambled on down the worn footpath to the creek, stopping only once to lean against a scrub oak and shake the sand from her shoes. The water was cold and tasted sweet, fresh, bubbling out of an underground spring buried far beneath the hills.

Beneath the earth was life, while the top of the land was dying, worthless and sometimes useless. On that afternoon, Barbara felt the same way. She dreaded the night. She dreaded tomorrow, but knew that both would come. She had no idea what either of them would bring. There would be no more pain. She was numb. Disappointments? She had gotten used to them. Hope? There was none. Not anymore. Not after seeing the ramshackle surroundings of her new home, if that's what it really was.

But then, in five years she would be eighteen. She could leave and be on her own, maybe even sooner. She would be free with nothing or no one to hold her back, and she would go as far and as fast as Rebel could take her.

Night crept slowly across the plains, coming down from the mesas to the west and following the shadows as they snaked their way through the canyons, easing the sting of the summer heat. Barbara sat on the apple crate beside the front door, watching the ribbons of darkness become entangled with the antenna wires, then move on toward the cornstalks, finally reaching greedily for the cement foundation, devouring everything that it touched. Beside her, Gabriel poured the bucket of cool water into an old hand-me-down galvanized washpan. He tossed his hat to the ground and began rolling up his sleeves.

"When did you stop building on the house?" Barbara asked, pulling her hair out of her face and tying it into a ponytail with a rubber band.

Gabriel leaned over the pan and splashed water in his face. "Thirteen years ago," he answered.

"Why?"

"Too big for just one man to live in." Water ran through his beard and dropped in tiny circles on the ground. He sighed. "An' not big enough for raisin' chickens."

"Well, you got plenty of room out here," Barbara told him.

The old man nodded and lathered his hands with soap, washing away the grit and the grime that Caprock had left in streaks upon him.

"So there's plenty of room for Rebel."

Gabriel grabbed an old towel hanging on a tree limb and dried his face. He wasn't real sure what he was going to do with the girl sitting there on his doorstep, much less a horse. At least, Barbara sounded like she had an awareness and a respect for the land. Maybe a little of his blood was flowing through her veins after all.

"That's what's important, Barb," he said.

"What?"

"Room." He tossed the towel back across the limb and threw the soapy water back under the mobile home. "I ain't got no use for folks breathin' down my neck," he said. "Just give me a few good acres of dirt. That's the only thing worth ownin' in this life anyway. Dirt. The sun can bake it till it cracks. The rain can wash it away. But can't nobody take it away from you. Even if all you own is a hole, it's got good, solid dirt down in the bottom of it...Yes, ma'am."

Sometimes, Barbara thought, Gabriel could sound like a preacher. But seldom did he ever act like one.

She stood, poured her water into the pot, and scrubbed her hands. "I need a towel," she said.

Gabriel nodded toward the soggy one in the tree. "Use that one," he replied.

Barbara, repulsed, rolled her eyes and looked away. "You got a dry one?"

"Why? You're just gonna get it wet again."

The girl wiped her hands on the skirt of her black dress and, without another word, stepped into the mobile home and slammed the screen door behind her. She rummaged around the kitchen, bumped into a chair and almost slipped on an egg shell before finding a kerosene lamp and lighting it. The wick blazed brightly, but unevenly, and shadows danced like grim puppets on the wall. The miserable shadows, Barbara decided, belonged to her.

Supper was all that was cold inside the cramped mobile home. Gabriel had opened two windows, and it didn't matter about the third one. It was already cracked. All he and Barbara could feel was the hot, dry breath of summer. They sat beside the old man's homemade table, a weather-worn barn door propped up on two saw horses, and dug into a couple of cans of beans.

When Barbara had taken them from the pantry shelf, she had asked Gabriel, "Want me to warm them for you?"

"It'd be a waste of time."

"Why?"

"I cook 'em after they've already hit my belly." He handed her a jalapeno pepper. "Just gnaw on one of these," the old man said. "It's hotter'n fire anyway."

"Do we have any meat?" Barbara asked, concerned.

"Sometimes."

"What do you mean?"

Gabriel grinned. "It all depends on whether you can find that piece of pork they stick in the can with the beans."

Now Barbara had propped her chin in her hands and was silently watching Gabriel as he sopped out the can with a piece of white bread. He was looking for the missing pork and not having very much luck in finding it. Suddenly the old man became aware of Barbara's stare. It gouged deep inside of him like a hot poker and it made him uneasy. He didn't like it, not for one minute.

He set the can abruptly on the makeshift table and growled, "Whatcha starin' at?"

"Nothing."

"I know when I'm bein' stared at," Gabriel snapped. "I've been trailed by a pack of wolves before, and I could sense them lookin' at me even when I didn't even know they were there." He paused, and his tone softened. "What's your problem?"

Barbara, flushed, glanced away. "Gabriel, why didn't you ever come to see us?" she asked.

"I came to your birthday party." Gabriel again attacked the can with the bread.

"My fifth birthday party. And you didn't bring me anything." It was not an accusation, just an afterthought, a painful memory that had become unlodged from a faraway corner of her mind. The words came tumbling out, even though she had never intended to speak them.

"I brought you a pair of overalls," Gabriel said quietly. He tossed the empty can toward a paper sack and missed, and the can rattled against the pipes beneath the sink.

"You didn't give them to me."

Gabriel shrugged, stood up, and shuffled across the floor, restless but not going anywhere. "I saw the dolls you had," he told the girl, his voice sanded down to a hoarse whisper. "An' the teacups, an' the colorin' book, an' the red ribbon for your hair. They were little girl things, an' I didn't have none of those. So I stuck the overalls back in the pickup and came home."

"You never came back."

"My mule got sick, an' I couldn't go off an' leave him. My corn was dyin' on the stalk. There was a lot of sick cattle out there that needed me tendin' to 'em. An' I was always having' to wait for the postman to bring me the new seed catalog."

He stared out into the night, afraid to face the girl, not wanting to relive the days he had put behind him and tried to forget.

"Besides," Gabriel said, sitting down and struggling to remove his boots, "your daddy never listened to me."

"I would have." The softness of Barbara's voice startled him. Her words hit him with the impact of a hammer. "I would have listened to you, if you had wanted me to."

She paused, and the kerosene lamp flickered as a gust of wind fell through the window and lost its way in the darkened room.

"Other kids had grandaddies," Barbara murmured. "I never had one. Not till now anyway."

Gabriel didn't answer.

He took the lantern and limped back down the narrow hallway to the far end of the mobile home, sitting down on his frayed army cot. A sheet was wadded up on one end of the bunk, and most of the feathers were missing from his homemade goose down pillow.

"Go on to bed, child," he called, and the words echoed back to where Barbara sat in the night.

99

"Where?"

She had looked around earlier and found no beds in the trailer.

"Any place you can find that looks comfortable," the old man answered, stretching out on the cot, still dressed in his shirt and pants. "Just don't take up much room." He sighed. "I'd let you have the bed, but these lumps are already used to my old body."

"What time do you get up?" Barbara asked.

"When I wake up."

"When's that?"

"Early."

Barbara forced a laugh. "Do you get up with the chickens?" she teased.

Gabriel grunted. "I wake up the chickens," he said. It wasn't long before Barbara heard him snoring, and it sounded as though a whirling dervish had been turned loose in the trailer, and it couldn't get out.

Inside a dresser whose scratches had never been touched with polish, Barbara located two sheets that didn't match and what was left of a horse blanket that had been rolled under too many saddles. She stretched them over a sofa that Gabriel had probably found lying in a ditch alongside the road. Surely he hadn't been foolish enough to buy it, she thought. Surely no one had been foolish enough to buy it. The velvet had been worn smooth and the embroidered flowers on the cushions had long lost their bloom. Once the sofa had no doubt been a dark, rich brown, but now it was the color of a stagnant stock tank, circled with pools of tepid water.

Barbara crawled beneath the sheets. Like Gabriel, she, too, remained fully dressed, and her face was twisted with disdain and embarrassment. It was awkward living elbow to elbow in a trailer so small she didn't even have enough room to change her mind, especially with a disgruntled old man who had the personality of a dill pickle.

Barbara shut her eyes, but sleep ignored her. Once she thought she heard Rebel screaming in the night but knew her mind was simply playing games with her, that it was probably the faraway howl of a coyote or a screech owl nesting close to the ground.

Down the hallway, Gabriel's snoring could easily be mistaken for a mule braying with a sore throat.

The girl smiled to herself and almost giggled. She tried to turn over on the sofa and stretch her legs, but it wasn't large enough. And her eyes wouldn't stay closed.

Finally Barbara decided that she couldn't lie there anymore. She was tired, bone tired. But the sofa certainly wouldn't let her rest. She ached between her shoulder blades. The top sheet had gotten tangled with her legs and no breeze at all was stirring to cool her face. The blanket still smelled of horse sweat, and the wrinkles in her dress began to hurt and pinch her skin. Barbara kicked the sheet away, eased off the sofa, and found her boots. Carrying them in her hands, she tiptoed to the screen door, opened it, and stepped out into the darkness.

Gabriel's snoring was caught short as though he had been shot at and hit. The squeaking of the rusty hinge had startled him. He opened one eye. Just outside his window, the old man could see Barbara shiver slightly as the clammy night air brushed against the perspiration that streaked her cheeks. She stuffed one hand into her pocket and pulled out a couple of jelly beans, popping them into her mouth as she sat down on the apple crate. The night was calm, and even the wind had lulled itself to sleep.

Sitting up on the cot, Gabriel opened an old trunk against the wall and took from it the brass framed photograph of a young girl. He stared at it as he had done so many times in the past. He didn't need any light to see the unruly brown hair, the impish smile, and the touch of freckles on her nose.

His vision was his memory. She was twelve, maybe even fourteen. He couldn't remember. But he had to admit to himself that she bore a striking resemblance to the little lady who was sitting by herself in the darkness outside his door. He held the picture as gently as a father would hold his child.

But then, all he had left of the child was the photograph.

He still had trouble believing that Miriam wasn't there when he called her name at night. Now another little girl was here. The years, or maybe it was fate, had dealt him an odd hand. And he didn't know whether to play it, fold, or just keep bluffing.

Gabriel looked again outside the window, at the unruly brown hair and impish smile and touch of freckles that almost glistened in the moonlight.

Maybe Miriam had never left at all.

The fairgrounds were sweltering beneath the furnace blast of a typical August morning. Even the wind had ceased to blow, and the heat hung above the arena like the smoke from a smouldering mattress with no breeze to push it around. Stinging. Oppressive. Stifling.

Barbara ignored the heat. She had grown up with it. She had her sights set on the last barrel, leaning forward slightly in the saddle as Rebel's hooves dug into the soft dirt and threw up a dusty spray as the big sorrel sprinted across the arena floor.

High in the bleachers, Sharon Wilson stood pouting beside her father. Her starched designer jeans had begun to lose their crease, and the sequins she usually wore on her shirt had been replaced by cotton fringe. Neither father nor daughter could take their eyes off the big horse below as he swung gracefully around the third barrel and galloped madly toward the gate.

"That," said Sharon coldly, "is the fastest horse in Caprock. Nobody can beat him."

"He's a fine one all right," Wilson agreed.

"He's the reason I'm in second place."

Wilson knew the reason why he and his daughter always clashed. They were too much alike. She had his competitive spirit and believed that his money could make anything possible. And it usually did.

"There's not much I can do about it this late in the season," he said. "All you have left is one race."

"One race is enough." She pointed to Rebel as Barbara led him out to the parking lot. "That's the horse I want," Sharon demanded. "That's the horse that can make me a winner."

Wilson frowned. "But Sharon," he said, "that horse belongs to someone else."

"It doesn't matter." There was no reasoning with her now. "He's the one I want. Get him."

"Maybe he's not for sale."

"Everything has its price." Irritation seeped from her voice. Her words were cold, confident. "Find out what it is. Then pay it."

"It's sometimes not that easy."

Sharon flashed a knowing smile at her father. "It's never been difficult for you, daddy," she snapped.

She turned and was gone. Wilson stared after her and sighed deeply. He had never failed her before, and he wasn't about to start now. Warren P. Wilson knew what he had to do, and time was running out on him.

In negotiations, winning was not always walking away with the best deal. It was walking away with what he wanted. Right now, he wanted a horse and wondered if Gabriel B. Spencer was really as tough and stubborn as he had always heard. Maybe the old geezer would even be willing to sell out cheap. A couple of thousand dollars would put Gabe on easy street, at least for awhile. And to Wilson, a couple of grand was only pocket change.

As he left the arena, Wilson saw Andy and asked her, "How's the girl making it?"

"She's not complaining."

"It's a shame," Wilson said sympathetically. "It seems like every break she's ever had has been a bad one."

"She's a tough little girl," Andy replied with pride. "But living with Gabe is like pouring salt on an old wound."

Wilson sadly shook his head. "It's gonna be real hard on her trying to keep up an expensive horse like that," he said. "I know how tight old Gabe is, and he's gonna have a coronary when he sees the feed bill."

"Gabe'll have a coronary when he has to buy an extra can of pork and beans for Barbara."

Andy laughed and Wilson smiled. The time just might be right, he decided, to buy a horse.

Caprock lay uncluttered upon the prairie floor, scrubbed by the winds and always wide awake by the time the first rays of sunlight flickered down upon courthouse square. Gabriel stood beside the curb and spat into the dust that the breeze was kicking up beside his boots. It was as though he were trying to get rid of the bad taste in his mouth, and perhaps he was.

He had just left the attorney's office where he had been charged good cash money to have the estate of James Atkins liquidated. About all James had that was worth anything was his truck, and it was sitting over at the junkyard. Of course, there was a little insurance money, but the lawyer wanted to stick that in Warren Wilson's bank. Gabriel only laughed at him. He would rather stuff the cash in an old oil can and bury it out in the backyard.

He stepped out in the street, dodged a pickup truck that rumbled past, and ambled toward Arnold's Feed Store. Wilson himself was waiting beside the front porch, and Gabriel didn't like the way he was smiling. There was just something about the look on Wilson's face that he didn't trust.

"Gabe," Wilson called. "I hope you have a minute. I need to talk over a little business with you."

Gabriel slowed his walk to a lazy shuffle. Wiping away the sweat that had collected on his beard, he asked, "You doin' the buyin' or the sellin'?"

"Well, sir, that depends entirely on you." Wilson was grinning, Gabriel thought, like a jackrabbit eating thistles.

The old man's eyes narrowed, and he stared poker faced at the rancher and businessman who had inherited most of the land around Caprock and had bought the rest of it. Gabriel pulled the brim of his hat down, shading his expression, and he made no reply. If Wilson wanted to do business, then Wilson could do the talking. The man who said the least, Gabriel knew, usually made the best deal. He propped himself up against the wooden rail beside

Arnold's feed store, pulled a frayed cigar from his hip pocket, and waited.

"Gabe, I realize you've got a problem, having that little girl move in with you," Wilson said, draping an arm sympathetically around the old man's bent shoulders. "It takes money to keep an extra mouth fed. I know. I got a little girl of my own. I don't know how in the world they can eat so much and still stay so doggone slim."

He paused, then lit up a cigar of his own.

Wilson continued, "Now I know you don't really have a place to keep that horse of Barbara's. I understand George Hendrix is wanting his barn back now that the girl's daddy is dead. He's gonna tear it down and turn all that land into a trailer park. At least that's what I hear."

Gabriel sighed, pulled out an old hand-me-down barlow knife, and snapped off a mesquite branch that hung over the sidewalk. He sat down in the dust of the steps and began to whittle, not even bothering to look at Wilson. "Well, you got the bushes beat flat, Warren," he said cautiously. "When you gonna get around to business?"

Wilson cleared his throat and his smile dimmed. "My business is horses," he said, shoving his hands into the pockets of his western-style suit pants. "I breed 'em, I buy 'em, I sell 'em — and I'm always in the market for another one." He knelt beside Gabriel and finally got to the point. "I have a place for that horse of yours. A good place. I can handle the feed bill, take a big load off your shoulders, and put cash money in your pocket at the same time."

Gabriel shrugged.

"You interested?"

"How much?"

"Say fifteen hundred dollars."

Gabriel bit off the end of his cigar and spit it into the street. "The horse belongs to the girl," he said.

Wilson smiled again and reached for his checkbook. "It certainly does," he said, "and she could flat use the money, too, being she's lost her daddy and all."

"Barbara and that horse are real thick."

Wilson stood and gazed for a moment at the thunderhead in the west that promised rain. There was a look of confidence on his face now. He knew the old man didn't have any use for the horse and probably didn't care much more about the girl. But he was horse trading, and all Wilson had to do was string him along.

"Gabe," he said, "me and you both know the horse isn't worth more than fifteen hundred dollars. But for Barbara's sake, let's throw in another thousand. Make it twenty-five hundred. What do you say?"

Gabriel tossed the whittled stick over his shoulder, leaned back, and rubbed his old, wind-cracked hands together. "I say it's a lot of money."

"Then we have a deal?"

"It ain't right me makin' Barbara's decisions for her."

A touch of irritation crept into Wilson's voice. "The court says that she's your responsibility whether you like it or not," he snapped. "And you know she's not old enough to know what's best for her."

Gabriel grinned but didn't let Wilson see him. Once a man got angry, he started dealing with emotion instead of horse sense, and the rancher was definitely getting a little hot under the skin.

"What you gonna give me to boot?" Gabriel asked.

"To boot?" Wilson frowned, wondering what kind of wool the cagey old man was trying to pull over his eyes.

"A sale ain't no good sale at all unless the seller comes out of it with a little something extra." Gabriel stood and stretched and felt his bones creak. He could smell fresh coffee brewing down at Hayes Cafe and thought that he had better get a cup before he went on back home. He turned to look at Wilson, eye-to-eye, and said frankly, "Me? I'm the seller. What you gonna give me to boot?"

"What do you want?"

Wilson's voice was cautious. He was on the defensive now. Gabriel was a simple man — but Gabriel had never fought fair. He was a hard man to deal with, so it was said. Wilson no longer doubted it.

Gabriel began walking down the sidewalk, limping a little more than usual, ignoring Wilson, glancing up at the clock on the courthouse wall. It was two o'clock, later than he had thought.

He heard Wilson shout behind him, "What do you want, Gabe? I'm ready to deal right now." He paused, and he became almost frantic. "What do you want, Gabe," he shouted louder. "Just tell me, and you got it."

The old man chuckled. Wilson wanted a horse, and he usually got what he wanted. But then, he had never done any horse trading before with Gabriel B. Spencer. Wilson was desperate. He had more money than sense. Well — he was out of his class. Gabriel would just let him stew awhile, then see what Wilson came up with.

For a moment, he felt sorry for the rancher, but, like a bellyache, the feeling didn't last for long.

How much was the horse worth, Gabriel wondered.

Chances were, he would soon find out.

Out at Gabriel's Three Eights Estates, Barbara gritted her teeth as she pulled the big barrel from the back of Andy's pickup truck and let it bounce to the ground at her feet. Her faded, checked shirt was stained with flecks of rust, and streaks of dirt had smeared her freckles. She wiped her hands on the back of her patched work jeans, stepped back, and looked out across the rugged vermilion hills that rolled into the distance beyond the trailer house.

Rebel stood patiently, tied to the lower branches of a mesquite tree, shaded from the late afternoon sun that threaded the hard-rock canyons with long, ragged shadows. Out in the pasture, she saw Andy carefully stepping off a cloverleaf pattern, marking it with caliche piles, and Barbara began rolling the last barrel toward her, moving across a barbwire fence that had fallen down and been left to rot.

When the third barrel had been stood in place, Andy looked up, smiled, and nodded toward the big sorrel horse. "See if it feels right," she told Barbara. And Andy watched the little girl run through the briars and brambles toward Rebel, her pigtails bouncing slightly on her shoulders.

Behind her, Gabriel's pickup truck chugged up the dirt driveway, spewing dust and smoke out across the sagebrush prairie, its motor complaining as usual, sounding a lot like a rusty hinge that hadn't been oiled. It slid to a stop beside Andy's borrowed horse trailer. The old man kicked the door open, climbed out and chewed angrily on his unlit cigar. He pulled his battered hat on tightly, using both hands, and stomped across the pasture as Barbara, astride Rebel, galloped past him and turned in toward the first barrel. The humor was gone from his eyes and his teeth were clenched tightly together. But Andy was paying no attention to him. She looked at her stopwatch as Rebel bolted toward the second barrel.

"What's goin' on?" Gabriel demanded to know.

Andy nodded toward Barbara. "She looks just like a grassbur stuck up on that horse," she said.

Gabriel snorted, not pleased at all. "Grassburs have been known to raise some pretty big saddle sores," he growled.

He grabbed Andy's arm, and, for the first time, she saw the anger that sizzled on the old man's wrinkled face.

"What do y'all think you're doin' out there anyway," Gabriel bellowed. He kicked a clump of cactus with the scarred toe of his boot and crumpled the cigar in a big, gnarled hand. "You ain't got no business out here."

Andy waited until Barbara had crossed an imaginary finish line, checked the time on her stopwatch, then looked up and faced the grizzled old man. "This is the first time Barb's ever had enough room for her own practice course," she said.

"It's my land."

"She's your granddaughter."

"Maybe." Gabriel turned away. "But I ain't sure I've

got enough room for her and the horse both."

He watched sullenly as Barbara pointed Rebel back toward barrel number one, pushed on by a competitive spirit that had obviously come from her bloodlines. The girl had seen her grandfather tramping out into the pasture, and she was spurred on by a sudden, almost desperate urge to impress him, make him proud of her. His approval was so important to her. She raced into the initial turn much too fast, cutting sharply, losing her grip as Rebel slammed into the barrel and reared in pain, pitching her headfirst into the rocks and thorns that cursed the prairie.

Barbara looked up, wiped the grime from her face, and saw the big sorrel stallion limping toward her. She was struggling to her feet, her stomach empty with fear, as Andy reached her side.

"Are you hurt?"

"No." Tears burned Barbara's eyes. "But Rebel is."

She dashed to her horse, stroking his big, thick neck as he nuzzled against her. Andy immediately dropped to her knees, checking the sorrel's foreleg, fishing a jar of salve from her jacket pocket. She gently brushed the blood away from the cut and applied a generous dab of the medicine to the wound.

Gabriel sat beside her, hurriedly pulling off his boot and peeling a thick, woolen sock from his foot. He took a match from his watch pocket, struck it with a broken fingernail, and set the sock afire, holding the smouldering blaze close to the cut and blowing smoke across it.

Andy frowned.

112

Barbara was looking at him as though she thought the old man had gone crazy or worse.

"Wool smoke'll stop bleedin' on a horse every time," Gabriel muttered. He looked at Andy. "Has the bleedin' stopped yet?"

The young county agent nodded.

"See." He grinned. "I told you it would."

Andy stood and defiantly folded her arms. "I put the medicine on first," she said, digging in her heels, unwilling to ever let the old reprobate think his homespun methods were more reliable than the one she had learned during four years of study in college.

Gabriel grunted and threw the burnt sock into the dirt, stamping out the last of the fire that burned in the wool. "That's why it took so doggone long," he snapped. "I had to cure your cure before the dadgum leg could start healin'." He picked his wrinkled cigar off the ground and stuck it back in his mouth.

Barbara glanced at Andy's unflinching black eyes, then at the amusement that had spread gently across her grandfather's face. She had grown tired of their petty quarreling. She leaned her head against the muscular neck of her horse. She was a child of the ranchlands and she had long known the realities of life in the west. Horses with broken legs couldn't survive. Men shot horses with broken legs.

"Is Rebel gonna be all right?" she asked. Her voice trembled, and Barbara waited for the answer she was afraid to hear.

Gabriel wiped the loose tobacco leaves from his beard

113

and the sweat from his forehead. "That horse has legs like cast iron," he said gruffly. "He's not hurt that bad. An' the smell of the smoke's bound to keep the flies away."

Andy reached out and touched Barbara's shoulder. "Just keep a close eye on him for the next day or two. He'll be all right and as fast as he ever was."

The muscles in Barbara's face relaxed, and she plucked a burr from Rebel's mane. He pushed his head against her shoulder, and Barbara dug into her pocket and found a jelly bean, slightly gritty, its sugar coating melted by the summer heat.

Gabriel turned to walk away, then suddenly stopped. Anger clouded his face. He spun around and said sharply, "If you hadn't brought that dang horse out here without askin' me about it, this wouldn't have happened." His eyes cut deeply into Barbara. She looked quickly down at the dusty prairie floor beneath her boots.

"But you said I could bring him out here when we had time," Barbara was pleading.

"I didn't have the time."

"Well, I did."

Barbara's voice was firm, as pointed as the prickly pear that lay in wait across the high plains. There was fire in her eyes. Her grandfather could be an ornery old cuss, but she could be just as stubborn as he was. After all, whether Gabriel liked it or not, she was a lot like him.

Andy, knowing when to keep quiet, knowing when to stay out of a family squabble where she didn't belong, discreetly backed away, moving toward her pickup truck as the long shadows of evening began to crawl toward her. "Excuse me," she said without expression, "but I think I'd better be going now."

"Might as well," Gabriel snapped. "You've already caused enough trouble around here." He didn't even bother to look her way.

For a moment there was silence, broken only by Andy's boots scraping against the rocks. She thought she knew when to keep quiet. She didn't.

"Gabriel," Andy said softly, "Barbara's only a little girl. Please don't treat her like a hired hand."

"I wouldn't think of it, Miss Andy." Gabriel grinned and leaned up against a twisted mesquite root fence post. "You have to pay hired hands."

He took his hat off and slapped it against his leg. The dust exploded off his pants. He saw Andy struggling to keep from fighting with him, trying desperately to control her temper. She had plenty to say all right but was, at least for the moment, managing to keep her thoughts and her words to herself. Andy pulled herself into the pickup and slammed the door. The engine wheezed, whined, then the truck roared down the driveway, the horse trailer bouncing crazily behind, kicking up dirt and rocks, spitting out smoke from a bad muffler across Gabriel's front yard.

The old man shuffled up to Rebel's side, reached up and scratched the big horse's forehead. He looked down at Barbara and squinted as the setting sun caught the corners of his eyes.

"It's not that I mind you havin' the horse out here on my place," he said, walking toward the dry wash that cut deep into the caliche earth. "It's just that I ain't got no place to keep him." Gabriel motioned toward the alkali foothills, topped with scrub oak and mesquite trees. "You can't just turn that horse loose out there. The varmints'll all chase him down. He'd be as helpless as a one-legged jackrabbit as soon as the cougars got hungry, and they're always hungry."

Barbara's hands tightened on the reins; her face paled.

"You don't really want either one of us," she said, her voice a whisper.

"I took you didn't I?" Frustration swelled up deep inside the old man. "I'm puttin' a roof over your head an' keepin' your belly full. What else you want from me?"

Barbara's face reddened with anger.

The confusion gripped her.

Gabriel took the half-chewed cigar from his mouth and chunked it toward a clump of scrub cedar. He turned and stomped toward the trailer, his place of peace and refuge until it had been invaded by a pint-sized ragamuffin whose freckled face was a constant condemnation of his own conscience.

Inside, the old man ripped his hat off and threw it in disgust against a wall that bore only a calendar that hadn't been changed in a dozen years. Gabriel sat down on the edge of his bunk and wearily placed his head in his hands. The gloom hid him but it did not comfort him.

In the distance, he could hear Barbara talking to Rebel, softly and sweetly, the way Miriam had once talked to him. How he had loved her. He missed her. He would never forgive Miriam for growing up without him realizing it.

116

10

The sun soaked into the earth around Barbara. Far away she heard the unanswered cry of a whippoorwill. It sounded as lonely as she felt. Lonely but free. Barbara glanced up and stared for a moment at the trailer. It was home. It was not where she belonged. Actually, she didn't know where she belonged. Not anymore. Sweat stung her eyes, her arms were sore, and the posthole digger had rubbed blisters on her hands.

Barbara had been working for hours on the rock and caliche dirt just behind the concrete foundation of the old dream house Gabriel had never built. Again and again she jammed the dull, chipped blades of the rusty posthole digger into the dry, cracked ground, jarred by the vibration that left her arms tired and almost useless.

Her hair was matted, her face caked with grime and grit. Overhead, a turkey vulture circled in a cloudless blue sky, riding the winds but going nowhere. Barbara stepped back to catch her breath and rolled up the sleeves of her red shirt. Behind her, Rebel stood patiently, tied to a mesquite tree that offered little shade from the heat of a summer morning. Barbara examined her fingers and saw that a blister had burst. She grimaced and dipped her hand into a bucket of cool well water, waiting, hoping the pain would go away.

Barbara sighed, again grabbed the wooden handles of the posthole digger worn smooth by years of use, and slammed them into a deep hole, striking rock. Sparks flew from the metal blades. The muscles in her shoulders ached. She knelt, her jaw clenched with stubborn defiance, reached down and tried to dislodge the cracked rock with raw, bleeding finger tips and broken fingernails.

"You diggin' for fish bait?"

The voice startled her. Barbara looked up into the wind-burnt face of her grandfather.

"Postholes," she answered.

"Findin' any?"

Barbara, tired and sore, threw the rock away in disgust. The work was hard enough. She certainly didn't need any old man coming around to harass her, she told herself. Barbara stood and scraped the dirt off her patched jeans.

"I figure a corral is the best way to keep Rebel away from those varmints you told me about," Barbara said, her emotion spent. "So I'm building him one. I can't keep him tied up forever."

Gabriel shrugged nonchalantly. "It's easier diggin' for

fish bait," he said.

"There's not anything easy out here."

Gabriel removed his jacket and tossed it over a mesquite limb. He took the posthole digger from Barbara's aching hands, and rammed its blades into the ground. Rocks flew, and they bit deep into the earth.

"That's right, Barbara," the old man said. "It ain't easy. It was never meant to be, and it gets tougher all the time."

"For everybody, or just me?"

Barbara sat down and began soaking her hand in the bucket of well water again, loosening the dirt from around the blisters that throbbed as though small hammers were pounding against her fingers.

"Nobody gets a break unless they inherit one," Gabriel growled.

"Like Sharon Wilson?"

"Maybe."

Gabriel grunted and brought another load of loose dirt out of the hole.

"It's not fair," Barbara muttered.

"Nobody said it was."

"Everywhere I go, all I ever have is bad luck."

Gabriel grinned. "That's better'n havin' no luck at all," he said.

The old man sat down beside Barbara and took her small hand in his. He squinted, then shook his head in an understanding sort of way.

"Wore a blister, didn't you," he said with a frown. "Ain't no horse worth a blister that big." Gabriel reached into his hip pocket and pulled out a small silver flask. "I got some homemade persimmon linament here that'll either take the sting out or the skin off," he continued. "I don't ever go far without it. Never know when I'm gonna need it. I usually need it two or three times a day. A couple of weeks ago I tore my hand on rusty barbwire."

"What happened?"

"I was halfway over the third strand when I realized it had four."

Barbara laughed, watching as her grandfather gingerly poured the homemade persimmon linament into the raw flesh. She flinched, then uttered a short scream of pain.

"Are you sure it's supposed to burn like that?" Barbara's eyes were wide, her suntanned cheeks pale.

"I don't know, honey," Gabriel said softly. "I always drink it."

He gently patted her shoulder with a rough hand and stood, bent slightly, his knees stiff and complaining about any form of hard work. Gabriel, without another word, picked up the posthole digger and again attacked the obstinate earth.

Throughout the afternoon, the old man, then Barbara, sank holes between the cracks of caliche rock. He swore under his breath as the pain began to creep into his joints, but Gabriel refused to slow down or take a break. The years had not dimmed the stubborn pride in his eyes, nor had they ever stood in the way of him doing any job that needed to be done, whatever the reason.

Barbara drew a fresh bucket of water from the well and watched as her grandfather washed the sweat from his dour face, then took a long, leisurely drink from his gourd dipper. His faded blue shirt lay plastered to his back, threadbare in the seams, and his black hat had grayed under a coating of fine, wind-blown dust.

"Thank you for helping me," Barbara told him.

Gabriel nodded.

"I didn't think you would," she added.

Gabriel shrugged wearily. "Might as well," he said, coughing to clear the dust from his throat. "It was too hot to chase snakes and too late to catch 'em. Besides, I figured if I didn't do something to help you fill up them holes I might step in 'em some night an' fall an' break a cigar or worse."

Gabriel was as blustery as a blue norther, but that's just the way he was, Barbara thought. His voice wasn't as harsh as usual, and she smiled. Gabriel was a hard man, but now and then, even he in an unguarded moment could be almost human.

Barbara, her blistered hand bandaged in a clean, white cotton sock, dug the last hole while the old man, using a double-edged axe, cut small cedar trees into posts. As the fading rays of an afternoon sun nestled in the crevices of a faraway hill, they stretched the final strand of wire into place. Gabriel leaned against the fence, and Barbara grabbed him by the arm, her face a mirror of excitement and satisfaction.

"We did it," she yelled.

"Well," Gabriel drawled, "at least I ain't heard the horse complain about it yet."

"He won't. He loves it. It's beautiful."

"It's crooked." Gabriel shut one eye and surveyed the

corral with a cocked head and a frown.

"It's good enough." Barbara remained undaunted.

"Yeah," the old man admitted. "It's good enough."

He suddenly felt tired and wasted, not quite sure why he had spent a day building something that the horse might not ever need. He remembered Wilson and the man's desperate desire to own Rebel. His offer had been good. It was going to get better, no doubt about it. It might even be too good to turn down. He watched Barbara run to the big sorrel, untie the rope, grab his mane, and, with a quick leap, pull herself onto his muscular back. Her smile, he thought, was as big as all of Texas. She didn't have much — there might come a day when she had nothing. Uneasiness flickered for a moment in his pale eyes, then lodged there.

Rebel, obviously eager for his daily exercise, bolted away from the mesquite thicket and dashed for open country as Barbara threw her arms triumphantly into the air and turned her face upward toward a sky that the coming night had streaked a dark purple. The sun had lit up the horizon with its last reflections of pink and gold. The evening star was a diamond that hung just above the silhouette of the treetops.

Gabriel stared at the big sorrel racing across the rolling pasture, his mane and Barbara's hair blowing loose and free in the warm wind. The girl bent low, urging Rebel on, even faster, through the mesquite and juniper. It was as if she was recklessly trying to outrun all the tragedy and grief that had haunted her life. Barbara and Rebel moved as one, a ballet of speed, grace and motion.

Gabriel ambled out across the prairie to meet them as the horse galloped toward him, covering the rocky pastureland with strong, powerful strides. Barbara reined to a halt and slid to the ground beside her grandfather. She was breathless. He scratched his face, and a clammy feeling dug deep into the pit of his belly.

"No horse runs the barrels faster'n Rebel," the girl said proudly, hugging the big sorrel's neck.

Gabriel wiped his sleeve across the beads of dirt and sweat on his forehead. "It's a shame to ruin a fine work animal by teachin' it to tiptoe around a bunch of painted oil drums," he said, and his words sagged a little.

"Barrel racing doesn't ruin horses," Barbara argued, the joy gone from her voice. "It's good for them."

"Maybe so," Gabriel replied. "Especially if you ever have to round up a bunch of barrels and drive 'em home."

He limped back toward the trailer house as Barbara, puzzled, gazed after him. The shadows of night were fast swallowing up the land around her.

She led Rebel into the homemade corral, packed the soil around the posts one last time, tested the gate to make sure it shut tight, then headed for her makeshift home as a lonesome coyote howled at the slender crescent of a new moon. A restless wind rustled through the dried beans that hung from the mesquite trees, and it smelled of alkali dust. Barbara kicked away the dirt that had caked on the heels of her calfskin boots and reached for the door. Inside, she found Gabriel opening a can of pork and beans with his barlow knife, dumping the contents cold and soggy on a pair of tin plates, left over from some

123

war Gabriel had fought in and forgotten. The old man turned and laughed at the sight that stood before him.

"I don't believe you left any dirt outside," he said, bemused. "I think you brought it all inside with you."

Barbara looked down at her grubby hands then retorted, "Daddy always said if a man didn't have dirt under his fingernails, then he didn't amount to much."

Gabriel raised an eyebrow. "That's one time your daddy was right."

Barbara poured fresh water into a dishpan and splashed it on her face and hands.

"He didn't like dressing up all the time," she explained. "He'd rather have been farming."

Gabriel set a plate of beans beside Barbara and lowered himself stiffly onto a wooden bench beside the table. "Trouble was," he said, "your daddy owned more of them fancy, two-toned neckties than he did land. An' he only had two of them."

"He was the best daddy in the world," Barbara whispered.

"I sure wish you'd known your mama."

"Was she pretty?"

Gabriel stared at his granddaughter and memories of the past clouded his eyes.

"You ought to know," he said.

"How could I. All I ever saw was a picture, and it was old and yellowed."

"Just look in the mirror sometime," the old man replied, "an' you'll see Miriam lookin' back at you."

"But she was all grown up."

"Not to me, she wasn't."

Gabriel sighed, removed his hat, and quickly, almost awkwardly, bowed his head. He nodded to the plate of cold beans before him and prayed, "Lord, it was yours. Now it's ours. Thank you for givin' it away."

"Amen." It was barely audible.

"Now, let's eat," Gabriel bellowed, trying to change the subject, trying to erase for a moment his thoughts of the little girl who had once followed him around back when life was younger and the times were better. She had trailed after him in the pastures like a tiny, freckle-face shadow.

"You should've let me do the cooking," Barbara said matter-of-factly.

"I been doin' my own cookin' for years."

"Maybe that's why you're so grouchy."

Gabriel frowned and snorted like an old bear. Barbara was smiling.

He started to reply, then stopped himself. She's got spunk, he told himself. She gets in the way and she's more trouble than a den full of cross-eyed armadillos. But she's got spunk.

The old man finished eating his beans in silence and threw the scraps outside for the varmints, or whatever it was he heard prowling beneath his window at night. He slumped onto his bed and was asleep long before Barbara blew out the kerosene lamp and crawled atop the lumps in his faded, hand-me-down quilt.

She heard Rebel moving restlessly in the corral and felt better because she was with him again. Her hands hurt, her shoulders throbbed. She tossed and turned in the darkness, cooled only by a shy wind that brushed against the perspiration as it beaded on her face. By the time she had wallowed out a comfortable place on the sofa, the sun had already cracked the West Texas dawn.

Gabriel's routine slowly changed. Barbara did the cooking and did it just fine, he thought, as long as she kept the peppers hot and the coffee thick. He gradually spent less time by himself and more time with her, watching as she coaxed catfish out of the shallow creek and teaching her the fine art of playing dominoes.

To Barbara, it seemed like the old man could produce, as if by magic, the old double five anytime and every time he needed it to score. She swore he had it marked, and Gabriel only grinned a lot and beat her every time he shuffled first.

When Lisa Madrone's barrel racing horse came up missing, it was Gabriel who was called on to track her down. Barbara treked out across the barren hills behind him, following as close to his footsteps as she could.

"Belle didn't come out of the pasture for her feed last night," Juanita Madrone had said anxiously. "We looked for her until it got dark, then waited for daylight. She still hasn't come in. She is about due to foal, and sometimes that means real trouble."

"Don't worry," Gabriel has assured Lisa. "Horses have done a pretty good job of takin' care of themselves for a long time. Besides, good range horses don't get lost. They're just hard to find sometimes. That's all."

But he knew that a foal was no match for a pack of

hungry coyotes. And there was talk around town that Luke had heard a cougar screaming down among the rock canyons. In dry times, when food was scarce, the varmints came scavenging close to town, and any newborn didn't stand much chance of survival.

Barbara ran among the prickly pear of a mesa top, then turned toward Gabriel and shook her head in confusion.

"After awhile," she said, "all these hills start looking alike. I feel like we've been going around in circles."

Gabriel stopped to rest, propping himself against a rock, mopping the sweat off his wrinkled forehead.

"That can happen," he told her, "unless you get to really know this land. Me, I've wasted so much time traipsin' across these hills that they're beginnin' to be as familiar as old friends."

Gabriel pointed toward a dry creekbed that meandered through the flats and disappeared back beyond the outer edge of the alkali foothills. "There used to be a little town over that next ridge," he said, scratching his chin as he dredged up an old memory. "But it died out 'cause the supply train never found it." He paused as he squinted into the sun and continued, "An' old Sam Bass buried some bank loot in a dry cave somewhere around here and spent the rest of his life lookin' for a mountain with a hole in it."

Gabriel shaded his eyes, bent low, and nodded toward a slender waterfall, virtually hidden by a canyon, reflecting a rainbow in the sunlight. "Right over there," the old man said reverently, "old Yellow Feather hid out for three months while the Texas Rangers looked for his scalp. He just kind of slipped back behind the falls and vanished off the earth. At least that's what they say. Nobody ever found Yellow Feather. Nobody ever heard of him again. Some folks can't find their way into this country. An' I guess that some can't find their way out."

"What do you think happened to him?" Barbara asked.

Gabriel grinned and lowered his voice. "I think old Yellow Feather's still in there," he whispered.

She giggled, and they moved on down the rocky slope toward the dry creekbed.

They found Belle standing in the shade of a narrow box canyon, her newborn colt, black with a white slash across his forehead, lying at her feet. He squirmed, but the strength had drained from his tiny legs, and he rested his head weakly on the ground. When the colt saw them, he struggled to his feet in fright, trembled, and fell back upon the rocks.

Gabriel knelt beside him, gently cleaned his eyes, and quietly examined the foal. "This young'un's got itself a real bad case of the scours," he said finally.

"Will he die?"

"He could have if we hadn't found him. Nature usually ain't got much use for a midwife, but sometimes it needs a little help."

Barbara gently stroked the colt's neck and brushed away the flies that had swarmed around him. "What can we do for him?" she asked.

"We'll get him back home and let Lisa feed him plenty of raw eggs," Gabriel replied. "He'll be well before he ever knows how sick he was."

Gabriel helped the colt to its feet, then hoisted it gently across its mother's back. He popped off his suspenders and fashioned a homemade halter. He slipped it over Belle's head and led her out of the canyon.

That night, Barbara dreamed of the colt and of a renegade named Yellow Feather who walked behind a waterfall one day and never came out again.

Barbara awoke to the muffled sound of a thump, then another just outside the trailer. She rubbed her eyes and sat up, trying to chase the last cobwebs of sleep away.

Thump!

She looked around to find she was alone. Gabriel's battered coffeepot was still cold and untouched.

Thump!

The morning sunlight slithered through a cracked window and flooded the room. Already the day was warm, promising to be even hotter than usual.

Thump!

Barbara pulled on her jeans, grabbed for a fresh shirt, and brushed the hair away from her face.

Thump!

From the doorway, she could see Gabriel raising the big double-edged axe above his head, then hammering, again and again, into the stubborn soil that held the old stump in place.

Thump! Dirt flew and splinters spun loose around his boots.

Thump! Barbara fastened the fake pearl buttons on her shirt and ran across the yard toward him.

Thump!

129

"How's it coming?" Barbara yelled loudly.

Gabriel swung the axe one more time before he answered. "If I was you, I'd put my money on the stump." He paused long enough to blot the sweat that creased his face. "Every doggone dime of it."

He tossed the axe aside and picked up a shovel, twisting the blade down amidst the knotted root system that clung greedily to the ground, scraping away the loose dirt.

"The stump's not in anybody's way," Barbara said as she yawned. "You ought to leave it where it is."

Gabriel stepped back, leaned on the handle of the shovel and gazed across the unkempt yard of his homeplace. A look akin to disappointment furrowed into his eyes.

"This place was all right when there was only one o' me livin' on it," he said, allowing his voice to grow softer. "I didn't have much, but it was more'n I needed. Now there's two of us. So I got to do some cleanin' out and cleanin' up. Might as well start with the land first. Lord knows it's been here the longest."

"Can I help you?" There was eagerness on Barbara's face. She began rolling up her shirt sleeves, ready to go to work.

Gabriel stared at her and frowned. She was only a wisp of a girl, and the stump was as ornery as a wild-eyed mule that didn't want to go anyplace it had never been before. He rubbed his jaw thoughtfully, then a grin broke out amidst the stubble of his beard.

"Can you drive?" he asked.

"Daddy used to let me sit in his lap on long trips, and I'd hold his truck in the road, and I never had any problems at all. Never."

"Well, then, let's see if you can handle a pickup the way you handle that horse of yours."

Gabriel dropped the shovel and turned toward the truck. His step even seemed lively as he walked to it, and Barbara swore she heard the old man whistling, even if she didn't know the tune. He eased the pickup back against the stump, climbed out of the cab, and announced with contempt, "This ornery old stump's bigger'n me and stronger'n me, but doggone, it ain't gonna outsmart me."

Gabriel quickly wrapped one end of a rusting old log chain around the stump and hitched the other end to the bumper of his truck, pulling it tight. He stood, wiped the grit from his hands, and motioned for Barbara to crawl into the pickup. She grabbed the steering wheel with both hands and strained to see above it. The windshield was so far away and so high. Barbara suddenly felt useless, but Gabriel wasn't perturbed at all.

"Well," he drawled, "it looks to me like your legs quit growin' 'fore they touched the floor, didn't they? Never mind. Just scoot yourself on down until they hit bottom. Ain't no use in you tryin' to look out the windshield. You ain't gonna see that much anyway."

Barbara shifted her position until her feet, at last, touched the floorboard.

"There's the clutch," he said, "an' there's the footfeed. Race the motor up real hot, an' when I holler, you mash this one and let up on the other one real easy like. With you pullin' and me pushin', that danged old stump oughta come out o' the ground like an abscessed wisdom tooth."

Gabriel put the truck into low gear and Barbara, wide-eyed and tense, stared ahead, flushed with anxiety. Butterflies turned somersaults in her stomach, and she waited to hear Gabriel's voice again. Her knuckles had turned white and she was sweating, but she knew it wasn't the heat.

The old man wedged a crowbar between a large rock and the bottom of the stump. He squared his feet, dug the heels of his boots into the ground, braced his shoulders, and nodded toward Barbara.

"Easy now," he called out. "Stretch that chain out as tight as you can get it before you gun it."

Barbara popped the clutch, and the pickup, its motor whining, crow hopped for a few feet, the tires digging into the earth, the smell of burning rubber piercing the air.

"Slow down, dadgummit," Gabriel yelled. "Slow down!"

The pickup made one last feeble lurch then gave up as the engine coughed and died. Gabriel checked the chain, stretched tight, then relaxed the grip on his crowbar.

"One more time, honey," he said calmly. "An' this time, give it all you got, then give it a little bit more."

Barbara, much too nervous to speak, nodded and fumbled with the key. The motor commenced grinding but refused to ignite. She scooted down, turned the key again, and the pickup roared to a start, shaking like a bucket of bolts about to jerk loose and spill.

Gabriel rammed the crowbar into an earthen crevice

132

beneath the stump. He bowed his back and strained against the metal rod, digging out a deeper foothold in the barren soil. His veins popped taut and blue, like wrinkled crow's feet, just under the thin skin of his temples. He gritted his teeth and chomped down hard on the cigar. The old pickup groaned, and the stump wavered. The truck's front tires lifted off the ground. It was might against might, the wanning strength of man and machine against a tangled mass of roots that had grown deep in search of water, had grown insolent in a land where only the tough had ever been able to hang on.

Dust kicked up into the old man's face and he could no longer see the pickup. He only heard it, a high pitch, a guttural growl as the rusty old engine fought to hold together and threatened to break apart. The rear tires tore into the earth, shoving rocks and dirt down the hillside and Gabriel felt himself losing his sweaty grip on the crowbar. He leaned harder, throwing his weight against the rod. The stump slowly began ripping its way out of the soil, pulling loose from a selfish prairie that had claimed it for decades.

Suddenly, it gave away completely.

Gabriel pitched forward off balance, landing face first in the hole. He looked up, blinking in the dust that felt like rocks in his eyes, and saw the pickup racing full speed toward the creek, the stump dangling helplessly behind.

Barbara's eyes were frozen on the terrain that sped madly past her. Her foot stabbed at the brake pedal and missed, and she again jammed the accelerator to the floor. She would have screamed, but didn't have time.

The truck swerved frantically, pointing toward a clump of mesquite trees that seemed to be rushing toward her. Barbara, fighting to regain control of her senses, as well as the steering wheel, cut the pickup sharply to the right. It veered sideways past one tree, spun around, and slammed into the trunk of a decrepit oak that had lost its battle with the years of drought. The engine sputtered once more, then died altogether. The only sound on the prairie was the dried, broken limbs of the oak scraping against the cab of the truck.

Gabriel, out of breath, a flicker of fear in his eyes, stumbled down the hillside and fell against the pickup, yanking open the door, looking down into Barbara's dust-streaked face.

She had bitten her lip until it bled. Her hands still gripped the steering wheel so tightly that her knuckles were white. A bump, a purplish bruise, was rising up on her forehead where she had been thrown against the side of the door on impact. Barbara tried to smile but couldn't find one. Her words came slowly.

"You were right, Gabriel." She sighed, her breath coming in shallow bursts. "It came popping out just like a wisdom tooth." Then pride crept into her voice. "We flat got it out of the ground, didn't we?"

Gabriel relaxed and allowed himself a grin. "An' we hauled it off, too," he replied. "Are you all right, girl?"

"My head hurts."

"You took quite a lick on it."

The old man took his granddaughter's arm and helped her step out of the pickup, holding her as she tried to stand on weak legs that had lost their feeling. Barbara glanced back at the truck and winced. The oak had left a ragged crease in the left fender, and the tire had been shredded into strips of bald, burned rubber.

"I tore it up, didn't I," she said, and for a minute Gabriel thought she was going to cry. "I'm really sorry. I tried. Honest I did. But I couldn't stop it till the tree stopped it."

"The tree did a pretty good job."

Barbara's downcast eyes turned away from him.

Gabriel patted her shoulder and squinted as he surveyed the damage. He leaned over the hood of the truck and ran his hand over the assorted numbers he had penciled in on the paint.

"It appears to me that the only thing you knocked out was the bill for birthin' Alfred Ray's calves," the old man told her calmly. He shrugged, "An' that don't make no difference. Alfred never gets around to payin' anyhow."

Gabriel walked around behind the pickup, casually unhooked the chain from the stump and tossed it into the bed of the truck.

"Don't worry about it, Barbara," he continued. "You did just fine. You scared the daylights outta me, an' you probably chased off every jackrabbit within cookin' distance of my stew pot. But you did just fine."

"It was just like the first time I rode Rebel," Barbara said, confidence returning to her voice. "I got beat half to death, but I didn't get throwed."

"That's what's important," Gabriel assured her. "When you win, that's fine. When you lose, that's fine. But one

135

thing this world won't stand for is a quitter."

"I'm never gonna quit."

Gabriel smiled. "No, girl," he admitted, "I don't believe you ever will."

He pulled an old hand-crank jack out from beneath the pickup seat and slid it under the truck.

"I'm gonna put another old tire on it," Gabriel told her. "You run up and bring me down the crowbar so I can straighten out this fender a little. Then let's you and me see if this ol' truck's still got enough gumption left to get us to town. There ain't nothin' that'll ease the pain of a little hard work like a couple of eggs down at the Hayes Cafe."

Barbara nodded and Gabriel leaned against the truck, watching her run back up the hill. She was just a little thing, but she was a lot like him. Maybe too much. He wondered what in the world he was going to do with her. He wondered how he could survive if he ever lost her again. For a moment, Gabriel was almost sure the flying pigtails belonged to Miriam.

11

Warren P. Wilson was a man who had always felt secure within the richly-furnished confines of his own office. It was his seat of power. When he sat behind that big, hand-carved, mahogany antique desk, wrapped in the leather cushions of his overstuffed black chair, the banker could be intimidating to anyone who had the misfortune to sit before him. He liked it that way.

Behind him, hanging neatly on the wall, were the papers that gave him authority to do almost anything he wanted to do in Caprock: the degree in business from Southern Methodist University, the past presidency plaque from the cattle raisers association, the Man-of-The-Year awards from the Caprock Chamber of Commerce, Lions Club, Girl's Barrel Racing Federation, county hospital, Daughters of the Confederacy and YMCA, as well as the autographed picture of the

137

governor of Texas shaking his hand during a campaign fund-raising dinner. It was all memorabilia that underscored Wilson's importance to his community and to his state, especially to small-time farmers and ranchers who had never even seen the governor in person, who felt like small fish in a small pond that had been dried up by the long hot summer.

Wilson always held their fate in the palm of his hand, or at least in the account books at the bank. He loaned them money to keep their operations running. He also had the power to foreclose and take their land away from them when hard times made it virtually impossible to repay a loan that financially shackled them. Wilson preferred to let people owe him with both money and gratitude. He liked to hold long-term debts, never knowing just when it would be advantageous to collect, but knowing the time would always come.

That morning, however, the banker wore a worried frown, uncomfortable with the problem that confronted him. Wilson always made sure he was in control of every situation. He gave orders; others followed and asked no questions. Now, someone else was telling him what to do, and Wilson found himself backed into a corner from which there was no escape. He loosened his tie, leaned back, and stared into the sullen face of his daughter.

"Daddy, I presume you have talked to Gabriel again about buying Rebel," she said.

"Not yet."

Sharon glared.

"But I will," Wilson continued quickly. "You have to

138

understand, horse trading takes time. If you make a deal too fast and easy, you can just figure that somebody's already stuck it to you. And bad. It's my policy, honey, that I don't trade unless I get the big end of the stick."

Sharon sneered. "We don't have time to waste horse trading," she snapped. "You either do something pretty quick or I won't stand a chance of winning at all."

Wilson sighed and glanced away. Outside the window of his office, he caught an unmistakable glimpse of Gabriel's old pickup turning onto the courthouse square.

"Don't worry, sweetheart," he said, reassuring her. "Your daddy won't let you down."

Sharon stood and leaned against the mahogany desk. Her voice was crisp, her words demanding. "This is the most important race of my life," she told her father. "If I lose it, it's all your fault. If I lose it, it's because you fooled around and didn't get me a winner to ride."

She turned and stalked out of the office, slamming the door behind her. She had left Wilson no choice and he knew it. He himself had always been accused of being a hard loser. But Sharon, he decided, was even worse. He smiled to himself and shook his head. Sharon was definitely his daughter. There was no doubt about it. Show me a good loser, he had once heard a famous man say, and I'll show you a loser. He definitely wasn't talking about Sharon. To Sharon, there was no such thing as second place.

Out on the square, Gabriel coasted into a parking place across the street from Hayes Cafe. As he and Barbara got out of the truck, the old man spotted Miss Hightower

139

from the welfare office cutting across the courthouse lawn toward them, and a tinge of irritation colored his face. Her hair was pulled back tightly into a bun, unruffled by the West Texas wind. Gabriel swore to himself that she must have had a penchant for eating pickles at the breakfast table, probably sour ones. Her face was pinched into a perpetual, self-righteous scowl, and she kept her nose tilted slightly in the air as though she smelled something bad and couldn't get away from it.

Miss Hightower stopped beside the curb and adjusted her glasses. Gabriel was dirty, but then she had expected that, the way he fooled around with horses and cattle all day. But Barbara, her eyes told her, was downright filthy. There was a bruise on her forehead and a tear in the elbow of her shirt sleeve. She certainly didn't look like a little lady. She didn't even look much like a girl. Miss Hightower made a mental note to file a report with somebody at the state office building in Austin.

She cleared her throat. "How are you and Barbara getting along, Gabriel?" she asked coldly.

"Fine, Miss Hightower. We're just fine." He forced a halfhearted grin.

The welfare worker straightened her linen jacket and turned to the girl. "Barbara," she said politely, "are you comfortable with your new home?"

"Yes, ma'am."

"I'll be out next week to check on you. We haven't forgotten, you know."

Barbara scratched her chin, looked up at Miss Hightower, and answered impishly, "Maybe you can

140

come Wednesday. I could sure use your help then."

"I'll be there."

"She needs somebody to hold the lantern for her," Gabriel interjected as he reached for a cigar.

"Why?"

"We gig frogs on Wednesday," Barbara said with mischief shining in her eyes.

Miss Hightower shuddered. Gabriel clicked his heels together and politely tipped his hat. Barbara winked at her grandfather.

"I'll be lookin' for you," he told the welfare worker. "Frogs won't hurt you none." He nodded toward Barbara. "She'll gig 'em. You skin 'em. And I'll fry 'em."

"It sounds awful." Miss Hightower bugged her eyes in disbelief.

"Yes, ma'am," Gabriel responded. "There's a lot of things around here that way."

By the time he had walked across the street, Barbara had already run into Hayes Cafe and was ordering biscuits and gravy with a scrambled egg on the side.

As Gabriel reached for the door, Wilson stopped him, took his arm and led the old man into the shade of the lone oak that spread its gnarled limbs above the cracks in the sidewalk. Gabriel pulled his hat down to hide his eyes, shoved the unlit cigar into his mouth, and waited for Wilson to speak. The banker's grin was much too big, he thought, and about as dependable as a three-legged mule plowing a two-acre garden.

"Gabe, I got a little testy the other morning," Wilson said, "and I apologize for it."

Gabriel leaned back against the tree and folded his arms, waiting for the banker to deal the cards.

"I still want that horse," Wilson said bluntly, "and I'm still willing to pay more than the going rate to get him. That twenty-five hundred, I believe that was the offer, will certainly go a long way toward making life a little easier for you and the girl. You can't argue with that, Gabe."

Wilson paused.

Gabriel chewed on the cigar and didn't answer.

"Times are getting hard," the banker continued, "and they're getting harder all the time. It's tough to make ends meet. Frankly, Gabe, I don't see how you and the girl are going to make it. Money's got to be getting scarce."

Gabriel pulled a handful of loose change from his pocket, held it in the rugged, calloused palm of his hand and studied it for a moment.

"Yeah," the old man answered. "If somebody gave me two dollars right now, why I'd have me two dollars and thirty-six cents."

Wilson reached into his coat pocket and brought out a stack of hundred dollar bills — new money — and he held it out to Gabriel. The old man slowly and reverently shuffled through the bills, then handed them back. His expression never changed; his hands didn't tremble, although they wanted to.

"That's security, Gabe," Wilson said.

Gabriel certainly couldn't argue with him. "Warren," he said at last, "you want a horse, an' I want what's best for the girl."

"The money's fair."

"For most horses, it is."

Wilson raised an eyebrow. "You wouldn't be trying to gouge me, would you, Gabe?"

Gabriel turned back toward Hayes Cafe. "I just always like to wait and see what a man's gonna give to boot," he called back over his shoulder. "Besides, it's against my religion to make a deal on an empty stomach."

Gabriel's scruffy beard hid his grin as he walked away from Wilson and ambled into the cafe. He knew the banker was still staring at him, probably frowning with disgust, and more than likely, playing with the gold chain that kept a gold watch attached to the pocket of his pants.

Gabriel surveyed the room with one quick glance and found it virtually empty. Barbara had found a seat alongside Andy at the counter. She was laughing and, Gabriel thought, it sounded real pretty when she laughed like that. Betty was frying eggs on the grill. It didn't matter how anyone ordered them, over easy, sunny-side up, scrambled, or poached. He knew she always fried them all the same way. Luke and Harmon were sitting at a back table, no doubt telling lies and maybe even believing them.

He paused beside the two men, reached down, picked up Luke's cup and took a sip of lukewarm coffee.

"I'm worried about you," he said to his old friend. "Your eyes look plumb wore out. A man who can't sleep has got something troubling his mind."

Luke nodded. "It's hawks, Gabe," he replied. "They're takin' all my chickens. I been sittin' up three days and

143

nights watchin' for 'em. But they never come close till I shut my eyes. It's like they're keepin' a better eye on me than I am on them."

"Get yourself an old muleshoe, Luke," Gabriel said, rolling up the sleeve of his yellowed shirt. "Stick it in the oven and leave it there. The hawks won't come around no more."

Andy whirled around on her stool. "Why that's the silliest thing I ever heard of," she blurted out, her eyes dancing.

"All I know," Gabriel told her without changing expressions, "is that I keep a muleshoe stuck in my firebox. I ain't had no trouble with hawks for years."

"Course, Gabe ain't got no chickens either," Harmon chimed in. He broke out in laughter, and it was contagious.

"I hate to tell you this," Luke said to Gabriel, "but the land and the varmints are gettin' wise to your old tricks. Times are changin', and you got to change with 'em. Now take Miss Andy here. She knows more than anybody how them college-educated professors raise a crop."

Andy's shoulders stiffened. She didn't know whether Luke was defending her, complimenting her, or making fun of her.

Gabriel leaned on the counter beside her. "Did they tell you to soak your watermelon seeds in sweet milk overnight before plantin' 'em?" he asked. "It's about the only way I know of to make the melon sweeter."

"Is that the kind of nonsense you're teaching Barbara?"

"If them professors didn't," Gabriel continued, "you

144

best get yourself a new set of books and use them old ones for fertilizer."

"That's all folklore."

"Maybe." His eyes were grinning at her. "But it works."

Andy cocked her head, folded her arms and asked critically, "And just what would you do to keep the green soybean leaves from turning yellow this time of year? Plant a horseshoe at the end of every fifth row?"

Gabriel lowered his eyes as though he was ashamed of her. "Why no man in his right mind would ever tell you to plant horseshoes, not with all of those poor horses runnin' around barefooted," he said softly. "What you do is take this wing feather from a two-year-old hawk, dry it over an open fire until the tips curl, wait until the second night of a new moon, then —"

Gabriel stopped in mid sentence. His attention, for the moment, was averted from Andy. Outside the cafe's window, he could see Wilson still pacing the sidewalk. There was a frantic urgency on his face. He was a man no longer in control of the situation. Gabriel sighed. He wanted to smile but couldn't afford to. He had baited Wilson and left him on the hook long enough. Now it was time to bring him on in.

"Excuse me, Miss Andy," he said without looking at her. "I've got some business that's callin' me." He patted Barbara's shoulder and shuffled toward the door.

"Don't pay no attention to Gabe," Harmon told the young county agent. "Gabe knows a lot about horses, but he don't know soybeans from Johnson grass."

"He thinks he does."

145

"He's just full of hot air. It's hard to catch, and you wouldn't have nothin' if you did."

Wilson watched the old man coming toward him, his shoulders stooped, a slight limp in his walk. His boots were scarred and the leather had split. His pants were threadbare, his shirt patched and frayed. Gabriel looked for all the world like a broken man who had been beaten down by too many burdens and misfortunes in life, a proud man who had never had much and who had lost hope of ever getting anything more. For just a fleeting second or two, the banker actually felt sorry for him.

"Gabe," he said tenuously, "I'm tired of talking money with you. Let's talk land."

Gabriel brightened. "I'll always talk land with you," he replied. "Land's the only thing around that'll still be around when man's long gone."

"We've been holding the note on those six acres of yours down at the bank for a long time now," Wilson said, opening the negotiations.

"You've owned 'em a lot longer than I have for sure."

"And how many times have I rolled the note over for you?"

"A couple."

"Nine, to be exact." Wilson's confidence had returned to his voice. He was dealing from strength now, standing on familiar ground. A smirk crossed his face. "Now I understand that you're four months behind on your payments again," Wilson said, pausing to let the words soak in. "I've been lenient in the past because I hate to see a man lose his home. I can't be lenient forever."

146

"You'll get your money, Warren." Gabriel felt annoyed and, for some reason, the sun seemed a lot hotter than it had before.

Wilson handed him an envelope. Gabriel opened it and drew out a set of folded legal papers, the deed to the acreage that was his last and most important possession on earth.

"I don't want your place," the banker said. "I'd rather have the horse. What you're looking at is the deed to your land, paid in full. It's yours as soon as I get the horse. That'll take a mighty big load off your shoulders, Gabe."

Gabriel stared off into space. He spoke as though he were talking only to himself. "It'll flat give Barbara something worthwhile to hang onto," he mused. "She ain't never had that before an' she deserves a little stake for the future. The land's gonna be here for her even when I'm not." The old man chewed on his cigar, shifted his weight from one foot to the other, and turned back to Wilson. "Warren," he said, his mind made up, "it's a deal if you put the deed to that land in Barbara's name. It should belong to her, not me. I've never had time to do anything with it anyway."

Wilson choked back a triumphant grin. He took the deed from Gabriel, scratched out the old man's name, and wrote in the name of Barbara Atkins. His hands were trembling with excitement.

"Let's get this change notarized to make it legal," he said. "You've made a wise decision, Gabe. This piece of paper's gonna give the girl a home nobody can ever take away from her."

Wilson began walking briskly up the sidewalk, but

Gabriel's voice stopped him. "Not so fast, Warren," the old man said crisply. "This deal ain't signed, sealed, and delivered yet. I'm gonna have to have that twenty-five hundred to boot. Horses don't come cheap, you know, especially now that it looks like I've just put myself in the market to buy another one."

The banker nodded, not surprised at all. He took a fistful of hundred dollar bills from his coat and handed them to Gabriel.

"It's all there," he said.

"I got no reason to doubt you, Warren." Gabriel stuck the bills in the inside pocket of his jacket without bothering to count them.

Now all he had to do was tell Barbara.

She ought to be pleased, but, he knew, a man just never did have any luck predicting what little girls or grown women would do. They had a tendency to get too emotional and lose their grip on common sense.

What would he tell her?

The truth.

Gabriel had never hid from the truth.

Barbara might miss her horse for a little while. He couldn't blame her for that. But in the long run, Gabriel told himself, she was a lot better off.

Still he wondered why his stomach felt as though a sore-tempered jackass had just backed up and kicked him hard.

He had to tell Barbara.

At the moment, he would rather have faced a barrel full of rattlesnakes with their feelings hurt.

12

The last color of the day lingered in the western sky, a blending of pinks and violets against the golden burst of a setting sun. The wind had died away on the prairie, except for a lone whirling dervish that kicked up loose sand and skipped its way toward the foothills, painted a deep purple by the shadows of twilight.

Gabriel leaned against a cedar post of the makeshift corral and watched Barbara slowly brushing Rebel's coat until it glistened like rich, red velvet. There was a closeness between horse and girl that he had not been able to understand.

Gabriel had in his lifetime had plenty of horses, as well as a few mules and a handful of old whitefaced cows. Now he couldn't remember any of their names. He wasn't sure he had even named them in the first place.

On the other hand, Barbara treated Rebel like family.

Didn't she know that God created horses solely to help man do his work, or get him someplace when it was too far to walk?

Uneasiness began to knot itself in Gabriel's stomach. He was a troubled man. He had always been a free man, an independent thinker who did what he wanted when he wanted, who didn't have to answer to anybody. For years he hadn't worried about anybody, including himself, and he surely hadn't worried about what anybody thought of him.

For years, he hadn't hurt anyone. But then, for years there hadn't been anyone around to hurt. Gabriel suddenly wished that when he had run off to Wyoming chasing the rodeo that summer he had stayed. If he had, he sure wouldn't be in the predicament he was in now.

Gabriel looked into the happiness that played across Barbara's childish, innocent face, and he felt the sharp edges of guilt digging away at his insides. He knew he had made the smartest decision about what to do with Rebel.

But was it the right one?

Regardless, he had to let Barbara know.

"You know, Barb, you're flat growin' up," he told her, not really knowing how to approach the subject he had begun to dread. "You're certainly not a little girl any longer. It seems like you've growed three years since you been with me."

"Maybe," Barbara answered with a smile. "But my jeans are still too big to fit right."

"You can't plan on playin' forever, you know." Gabriel rubbed his chin and stared across the prairie without

150

seeing it. "You got to start thinkin' about the future sometime, when those barrels are old and rusted and throwed away."

Barbara shrugged. "I'll get new ones."

"Just always remember one thing. As long as you got a little land to call your own, you don't ever have to take a back seat to anybody."

"I never have anyway."

Gabriel cast his eyes to the ground, then at Barbara. "I just want you to know," he said softly, "that I did what I thought was best. That's all."

Barbara stepped back from Rebel and turned to face her grandfather, a question mark in her eyes.

"What did you do?" she asked.

"What I thought was best, girl." His words were barely audible. "An' you deserve a lot more. I just wish I had it to give you."

His shoulders slumped, his face sagged, and the fire was gone from his spirit. At that moment, Barbara noticed how old and how fragile her grandfather really looked, and that surprised her. She had never thought of him as either old or frail before. Then he walked away, leaving her puzzled and confused. He seemed so uncomfortable and unsure of himself, which wasn't like the Gabriel B. Spencer she knew at all.

The old man went to bed without his pork and beans that night. He didn't eat at all, said he wasn't hungry. Barbara slept restlessly, tossing and turning, waking every few minutes, an uneasy premonition in her head that told her something was wrong. She just lay in the heat and darkness, staring out a cracked window pane, watching the stars until they faded into the faint light of dawn.

A noise outside startled her. When she opened her eyes, she saw the fresh rays of early morning sunlight being spun into a spider web above her makeshift bed. Had she been asleep after all? Barbara didn't think so.

Then she heard the throbbing rumble of a truck's engine as the motor idled, a door being slammed shut, footsteps in the yard. Barbara wiped the sleep from her eyes. Had she been dreaming? If so, the noise outside definitely had not been a part of it. There it was again, the unmistakable sound of a horse's hooves stamping angrily on a wooden trailer floor, and Rebel screamed with unbridled rage and fury.

Barbara sat upright and scrambled for her jeans with trembling hands.

Through the window, she saw her big sorrel locked away in Warren Wilson's own customized horse trailer, sky blue with a silver trim. Grady was nonchalantly climbing back into the cab of the truck, in no hurry, not even attempting to hide his face.

Barbara, fumbling with buttons, flung herself against the door, screaming, *"No!* Come back here. You're stealing my horse. *Come back!"*

Grady didn't hear. He pulled the door shut and shifted the truck into low gear. The engine began to growl and the tires bit into the caliche soil.

Barbara bolted barefoot into the yard, racing toward the truck and trailer that was pulling steadily away from her. Rebel was screaming. Barbara was screaming. Both in anger and in anguish.

Then she felt Gabriel's strong hand on her shoulder. Barbara leaned on him and grabbed his arm, but her eyes kept following the trailer that has been virtually swallowed up by smoke, dust and distance.

"Gabriel, Rebel's gone." Her voice was shaking. "They've taken Rebel. Mr. Wilson's stolen him. We've got to go after him. They've got my horse."

Barbara turned to run, but the old man took her arm in a firm grip and stopped her.

"The horse belongs to them," he said.

"What?"

Barbara was stunned. She couldn't believe what she had just heard. It was incredulous to think Rebel belonged to anyone but her. It didn't make sense. Gabriel must be lying to her. He had to be. Rebel was her horse, a gift from her daddy, the last one he had ever given her. And nobody was ever going to take Rebel away.

"The horse belongs to them," Gabriel repeated. He sighed and looked away. "I sold him to Wilson. I tried to tell you last night, but just never got around to doin' it."

"Let go of me."

"Listen, child."

"Let go!"

"Barbara clenched her teeth and tried to tear loose from the old man's grip, but Gabriel held to her.

"You don't have the right to sell my horse," the girl yelled. Her eyes smouldered with rage.

"Maybe not," Gabriel yelled back. "But I did what I

153

thought was best."

"Let go of me," Barbara ordered. "I don't belong here. I don't belong with you. Not anymore. I belong with Rebel, wherever he is."

She attacked Gabriel, screaming and crying, pounding him with her small fists, kicking at his knees, striking out in anger and frustration. He put his arms around her and held his granddaughter close, flinching as her wild swings found their mark, knocking his hat into the dust.

"I just wanted you to have a home," Gabriel tried to explain.

"I don't want a home." Barbara's words dug into him like a dull knife. "And I don't want you. You sold my horse and I hate you. Let go of me. I gotta get Rebel back."

"It's too late, child."

Gabriel released his grip, and Barbara backed slowly away from him.

"Rebel's all I had, and you sold him."

"I tried to do what was best."

"You never cared about me. You never cared about any of us." She wiped the dust from her eyes and tried to spit the sour taste out of her mouth.

Gabriel chewed on his own words, then swallowed them.

Barbara stared at him. Her breath came in short bursts of agony. Her chin quivered and tears streamed down her freckled face.

"I wish you had never come to get me," she hissed. "I wish you had just left me alone. I wish you were dead."

154

Gabriel nodded.

"You stole my horse," Barbara accused him. "I trusted you, and you stole my horse."

Gabriel picked up his hat and sat down, leaning against the trailer.

"All I did was make sure nobody'd ever take this place away from you," he said. "It ain't much. But it's yours. An' I got enough cash to boot so's you can buy all the horses you want. I shoulda told you about it last night."

"Rebel's the only horse I want."

"That horse won't be around forever. This land will."

"I don't want your crummy old land."

Gabriel reached for a wrinkled cigar in his pocket, stuffed it into his mouth, and this time he lit it. "Nobody handed me an' you life on a silver platter," he said, his gaze steady and without compromise. "We gotta scratch to get what we get. But we gotta scratch together or we ain't gonna get nothin' at all."

Barbara looked for a long time down the dirt driveway where the dust had settled back to the ground. It was empty.

"Daddy bought me Rebel, and he believed we could win the championship," she said, her voice strangely distant and hollow. "And we could have won it, too. But you stole it from us. You stole everything from us. I'd have been better off living anywhere but here."

Gabriel stood and dusted off the seat of his pants.

"What's done is done, Barbara," he said as gently as he could. "If I hurt you, I'm sorry. But just remember, if a horse stays down too long, he can't get up again. People

155

are no different. You can sit around here feelin' sorry for yourself, or you can start livin' the rest of your life."

"I don't want to live it."

"Suit yourself."

Gabriel walked back into the trailer and let the screen door slam behind him.

Barbara headed out into the pasture that had become so familiar to her, surrounded by the perfect pattern of a cloverleaf, dug deep into the earth by Rebel's flying hooves. When she closed her eyes, she could almost hear them striking the ground. She called Rebel's name aloud, but her words died in the warm wind that touched her face and dried her tears. Barbara sank to the ground, a portrait of solitude and heartbreak. She tilted her head back against the first barrel in the turn, the money barrel. She buried her bare feet in the cool loose dirt and let the hot day of summer pass without her.

13

Andy Beck walked with hesitation out across the sandy loam of the arena floor, not quite believing what she was seeing. Something was wrong.

Sharon Wilson, a radiant smile on her face, had come through the gate leading a horse she had never ridden before. She was tightly gripping the reins of a big sorrel. Not Diamond Cutter, but Rebel. He was dancing nervously behind her, snorting, pawing the ground, tossing his head, rebelling against the unsure, unfamiliar hands that held him.

Andy glanced quickly around the grandstand, searching for some sign of Barbara. There was none. She then turned back toward Sharon, unable to hide the bewilderment in her eyes.

"Don't look so surprised, Miss Beck," the girl said as the blue sequins on her blouse glittered in the morning sun. "Rebel belongs to me."

"Where's Barbara?"

"I haven't seen her."

"Where'd you get Rebel?"

"Daddy bought him for me." There was a smugness in her voice, an awareness that those with money always got what they wanted, and Sharon had never been bashful about flaunting her father's wealth.

"Does Barbara have a horse to ride now?" Irritation accented Andy's words.

Sharon shrugged. It was obvious that she neither knew nor cared.

Andy rolled up the sleeves of her red shirt and squinted into the sun. "It's not right," she said. "You shouldn't be switching horses with only one race to go."

"There's nothing in the rules that says I can't." Sharon spit out the words. "This is the year I win. The championship is mine, and nobody can take it away from me."

"Barbara has a chance."

Sharon laughed. "Not if she's walking, she doesn't." She mounted and turned Rebel toward the first practice barrel, fighting hard to keep him under control as the big horse bolted foward with a surge or power that she had never felt before. Sharon fought to manage him, but Rebel was running wild, headlong toward the barrel. She reached for her quirt, but the sorrel suddenly veered to the left, and Sharon dropped it, frantically hanging on with both hands as Rebel tore across the arena floor.

Outside the arena, Gabriel turned his pickup into the

parking lot, skidding across loose gravel and bouncing toward Warren P. Wilson's horse trailer, freshly washed, glistening in the sunlight. He saw the rancher reach for his car door, and the old man, his eyes determined and uncompromising, slid his truck to a stop beside the black Cadillac. Gabriel was talking before his feet hit the ground.

"Wilson," he yelled as he jammed the unlit cigar into his mouth, "I've thought it over. You can't have the horse."

The rancher smiled and straightened his brown suede jacket. "We've already shook on it, Gabe." His voice was apologetic, but not sincere.

"I want to buy him back."

Wilson eased himself behind the steering wheel, tilted the brim of his hat to shade his eyes, and leaned back in the plush leather seat. "A deal's a deal, Gabe," he said, turning the key in the ignition. "Besides, that horse is the only thing that's standing between you and my foreclosing on your land. Be thankful you had him. If you hadn't, you'd be back on the road, sleeping in the bed of that thing you call a pickup. And no telling what would happen to Barbara."

He drove slowly away, but Gabriel grabbed the window, running alongside the Cadillac, his face red, his eyes desperate. "You won't lose a penny, Wilson," he yelled, out of breath. "I promise you won't lose a penny, 'cause I ain't spent any of it yet."

"Gabe," Wilson said smugly, "you may be a horse trader, but you certainly don't know a good deal when you make one."

He picked up speed and Gabriel lost his grip on the window. The old man pitched forward onto the dust and gravel. Wilson never bothered to look back, and Gabriel thought he heard him laughing. He looked down at the blood on his hands where the rocks had torn his skin.

Andy Beck found him sitting in the shadows on the far side of the grandstand, alone and out of sight. At the moment, he seemed to prefer it that way. To her, Gabriel looked more haggard than usual, a sympathetic figure, but that did nothing to temper the anger that swelled up within her.

His trousers were patterned with dust, his frayed white shirt was stained with sweat as it clung to his back. His hat was propped up on his knee, and the cigar hung crookedly from his mouth. Andy decided that Gabriel was a man who had lost his last friend and deserved to.

She put her hands on her hips, leaned over, and snapped her words coldly, "Gabriel, what in God's name do you mean selling that little girl's horse?"

"I've been tradin' horses for a long time," the old man answered defensively. "That's my business, and I'm pretty dadgummed good at it."

"Maybe." She sat down beside him and pushed away the hair that the wind had blown into her eyes. "But you don't know anything about little girls."

Gabriel's back drew rigid. He had no patience with anybody interfering with anything he did, regardless of whether it was right or wrong.

Andy nodded toward the arena floor and continued,

"There's a girl sitting up on a horse down there that, by all rights, shouldn't belong to her. Why?"

"Because her daddy's got a lot of money."

"Or maybe it's because she's still got a daddy."

Gabriel shifted his weight uneasily. "This is our life," he said bitterly. "You may not like it. You may not think it amounts to much. You may be right. But you sure ain't got no business buttin' into it."

"Somebody's got to look after Barbara," Andy said. The glare in her eyes was suffocating.

"The judge gave me that responsibility."

"The judge made a mistake."

Gabriel jerked his head around and stared hard at Andy, chewing furiously on the cigar. His ability as a grandfather, a provider, a surrogate parent was being questioned. He didn't like it and would have fought if Andy hadn't been a woman.

Andy's voice softened. "Don't you realize that horse was Barb's whole life?" she asked. "Rebel was the most important thing in the world to her."

"Let me ask you a question," Gabriel said slowly. "How come them that yell the loudest and longest ain't never the ones that pay the rent and put the groceries on the table?"

Andy turned away.

"Rebel was all she had," she said quietly.

"She's got me."

"Then she doesn't have much to brag about."

Gabriel stood and shoved the cigar back into a worn pocket. "You're probably right," he replied as he limped down the wooden steps and out the back gate.

The silence around Andy was broken only by the sound of running horse hooves as they pounded, again and again, into the dirt of the arena floor below. She glanced down at the eager, laughing faces of her barrel racers. Most were simply excited about the chance to compete. They didn't expect to win, but they loved having the opportunity to try. A few worked hard to ride into the winner's circle. One would do anything to be a champion. And one, Andy sighed with a sense of loss and disappointment, was missing.

The days in Caprock moved as slowly as did the tepid waters down in Casita Creek, green and stagnant, going nowhere and probably never getting there. That was pretty much the way Barbara felt, too. She had been sitting on the bank for hours, her back against a gnarled mesquite tree, watching the scattered herd of white-face cattle foraging for what sprouts they could find on a prairie baked hard and sapped dry by the summer sun.

The tears had long since dried on her face but not in her heart. Everyone, everything she had ever loved had been taken from her. Her life had been disrupted, then shattered. She had had only one dream left, and now it was gone.

The late afternoon caught Barbara ambling slowly down a dirt road that cut through ungrazed pasture land. She seemed to be wandering aimlessly through the brakes, a little girl lost, astray or adrift within the lazy confines of summer. She knew where she was going, though she refused to admit it to herself. There was no reason to go. She knew she shouldn't go. But somehow, Barbara just couldn't stay away.

The heat was as prickly as desert cactus, but she was used to it. The red bow in her hastily-tied ponytail had come loose and the ribbon was fluttering in the wind. She wore her shirt tail out. The heel had broken on her right boot when she slipped and tumbled into the rocks of a dry ravine, making her walk with a limp.

When the night settled down around her small shoulders, Barbara sat on a bare knoll overlooking Warren Wilson's ranch house.

A new moon hung in the southern sky and the ground was devoid of shadows. The land beyond her was empty and foreboding. A coyote barked in the distant darkness.

Barbara eased her way cautiously toward a long row of white stables behind the main house. She ran quietly across the driveway, then hesitated, looking back over her shoulder as a truck turned suddenly through the gate. She leaped for the cover of a fallen barrel to dodge the headlights that probed the night beside her. Lying flat on her stomach in the grass, Barbara saw Grady drive his pickup past, following a winding roadway toward the bunkhouse he called home.

She could make out the faint sound of his footsteps in the gravel, waiting until she heard his front door slam before crawling out of her hiding place and slipping into the runway that led her down among the stalls. They smelled of fresh hay. Barbara patiently searched each one until she found Rebel, munching from a bucket of fresh oats that had been set on the ground at his feet.

The big sorrel jerked his head up, cocked his ears, and whinnied softly when he saw her. Barbara quickly unlatched the stall gate and stepped inside as Rebel gently nuzzled against her, his nose sniffing her shirt pocket, looking for the jelly beans he knew she always carried there. Barbara laughed, and for a moment it seemed to her that nothing was wrong. She was, at last, where she was supposed to be: with her horse. She wouldn't let herself believe that she would ever have to leave.

Barbara gave Rebel a handful of jelly beans and laid her head wearily against his thick neck. "I bet you've been missing these," she whispered. "I've sure missed you."

Barbara turned and took the lantern off the wall, lit it, then hung it back up and a strange array of cobwebbed shadows danced like ebony butterflies about the stall. In the dim light, she found a curry comb and began brushing the big sorrel's coat. Around her, she heard the dull thud of horses moving restlessly throughout the stables, but she ignored them, then forgot them, interested only in the one she loved.

"Are you lonesome fella?" she asked as she scratched Rebel's ears. "Is Grady taking good care of you? I know he is. He understands horses, even if Sharon doesn't."

She paused, and the tears stung her eyes.

"I'll be out there Saturday watching you win that championship," Barbara continued. "And I'll be awful proud because you won most of it with me."

The sudden sound of a bucket clanging against the outside walls startled her.

She heard the unmistakable, raspy voice of Grady,

angry and upset at himself for stumbling in the darkness and tripping over the bucket he had left lying beside the driveway.

Fear gripped Barbara. She wanted to run, but it was too late. There was no place in the stables to hide. She thought Grady had turned in for the night. It had never crossed her mind that he would be checking on the horses one last time before calling it a day. Maybe he had seen her lurking in the shadows as he drove to the bunkhouse. Maybe he had caught a glimpse of the light glowing in Rebel's stall. It seemed so dim to Barbara. It would look so bright from the outside.

She reached for the lantern, lost her balance, and fell from the gate, knocking the light to the ground. Rebel jerked back and instinctively kicked the lamp, breaking it, screaming nervously as it became a deadly torch amidst the piles of dried hay. The sparks flickered for an instant, then showered across the stall. Flames leaped toward Barbara like the hot, red tongue of a snake.

Lying on her back, she rolled away from the frantic hooves that pounded and pawed the earth around her, struggling to free herself from the fire that had engulfed the barn, trapping her and the horse. Crackling embers bit into her flesh. They felt like the sharp end of a leather quirt, cutting deep, and the air became thick with smoke, oppressive and suffocating, and she heard the big sorrel scream again. He reared back on his hind legs, his front hooves jabbing at a sheet of flame from which he feared he could not escape. The horse stumbled and fell heavily against the stable walls that held him.

Barbara coughed. Her lungs ached for fresh air. With her bare fists, she beat out the fire that crept toward her face, oblivious to the pain, fighting for survival, desperately kicking open the gate and crawling after Rebel as he bolted for freedom and raced into the night.

The cool night wind slapped Barbara in the face as she tumbled out of the black smoke that was boiling up from inside the stables. She coughed again. Her eyes were burning and swollen.

She wiped away the tears, suddenly aware of the frenzied screams of frightened horses, sounds that chilled her. They were imprisoned by fire and smoke and could be dying, Barbara told herself, and it was all her fault. Without hesitation, she turned back toward the stalls just as Grady's big hand grabbed her shoulder.

"What are you doing here?" His words were as sharp as a pistol shot.

Barbara pulled herself loose from his grasp and ran back headlong into the smoke, shielding her face with her arms, choking, coughing, groping in the darkness for the latches that would open the gates where the horses were held captive. Grady quickly followed her, dodging the angry fingers of fire that reached for them as the wind pushed the blaze toward the far end of the stables.

There was no time for questions or for accusations. They had to move fast, working together, or lose the animals that were striking out in fear, blinded by the smoke, fighting for their lives in the midst of the spreading wall of flame that stretched out toward them. The wood crackled as paint peeled back from the searing heat, and the roof exploded, then fell in smouldering ruins. Again and again, the girl and the cowboy battled their way through the fire, ripping the hooks from the latches, ducking to avoid the fury of flying hooves that kicked past them.

As the last horse galloped out of the stalls, Barbara, her face blackened by the smoke, streaked by tears of panic and guilt, stumbled backward into Grady's arms. She looked up, her hair singed by the flames, and blurted out, "It was an accident, Grady. I didn't mean to. I swear it. The lantern fell and broke and the next thing I knew the barn was on fire."

"What were you doing here in the first place?" Grady didn't wait for an answer. "You got no business trespassing around somebody else's property."

"I came to see Rebel." The cowboy's firm grip was hurting her.

"He doesn't belong to you anymore."

Grady's words cut deep. They returned her to the grim world of reality.

In the distance, Barbara could hear the wail of sirens as fire trucks sped toward the blaze that threw streaks of red and orange into the night sky. There would be policemen with them, she knew, and fire officials and all sorts of authorities asking all sorts of questions, blaming her, accusing her. There would be no one around to defend her, not now, not any more. Once they had all been friends, but that seemed so long ago. Now they would be as strangers, judging her, condemning her. She couldn't face them.

She broke and ran.

Rebel was waiting for her just beyond the barn. Barbara grabbed his mane, swung easily onto his back, and the big sorrel barreled past the burning stalls and disappeared on a dead run into the darkness of the prairie.

Within an hour, the flames had all died away, and the ground had become a quagmire of mud, soaked thoroughly by the hundreds of gallons of water that had been used to control the fire. Sheriff J.T. Rodriguez rummaged through the ruins, pausing every now and then to dig a scorched bit or stirrup ring from out of the ashes. He studied each item closely, diligently searching for the cause of the fire, before discarding it. The firemen tramped through the stalls in oversize rubber boots, dripping with water, checking to make sure the last ember had been doused, rolling up their hoses as they went.

Grady removed his hat and wiped the smut from his face with a torn shirt sleeve. His shoulders sagged wearily as he ambled toward Andy who was examining a chestnut that one of Wilson's cowboys had rounded up and brought back to the barn. Her hair was tangled, her skin smudged, and her jeans were stained with patches of water and mud.

"It looks like they've got the fire pretty well smothered out now," Grady said. "How are the horses?"

Andy stood and forced a tired smile. "They all appear to be in real good shape, considering what they've gone through. They're scared, but not hurt."

"I appreciate your coming out to help us like you did."

"I'm just glad I was home when you needed me."

Grady leaned back against the fence and propped his right boot up on the bottom plank. "I guess it could've been worse," he said gratefully. "We could've lost a lot of good horses."

"Wilson's lucky." Andy wiped her hands on her jeans and took a cup of coffee that a fireman was passing around. "Did anyone ever locate him?"

"Jake finally ran him down at the country club. They had some kind of dance going on. He'll probably come blowing in here at any moment now. Mr. Wilson flat ain't gonna like what he sees."

Gabriel, the wrinkles in his face as worn as his clothes, came leading a skittish, wild-eyed appaloosa to the fence, handing the reins to Grady.

"Here's the last horse that nobody could account for," the old man said, slumping against the barn door. "He looks like he got tangled up in a little barbed wire. He's got a few scratches, but they don't appear to be too bad."

"I'll look him over." Andy's voice was authoritative, and for once Gabriel was too tired to argue. She knelt and gently brushed away any traces of dirt and dried blood from the cut.

Behind them, Wilson's black Cadillac roared up the driveway and came to a stop on the loose gravel. The rancher leaped out and ran toward the circle of fire trucks, his face flushed with concern, heat, and anger. He stood for a moment, his eyes quickly surveying the damage, then turned to Grady.

"What's the assessment?" he asked.

"I'm afraid the stalls are totally wiped out."

"We lose any horses?"

"One."

Andy and Gabriel whirled around, surprised.

"I thought we had rounded up all the horses you had sleepin' in there," Gabriel said.

"Rebel's gone."

"Rebel?" Wilson spit on the ground in disgust.

"Yes, sir." Grady sighed, then continued, "Barbara took him and high-tailed it out of here."

"What was she doing out here?" Wilson asked coldly.

"She's the one who started the fire. Said it was an accident, and it probably was." Grady paused, then added, "She stayed and helped me free the horses before she took off."

Wilson stared at the ruins, his jaw set in anger. "Grady," he said at last, "get every hand we've got here as soon as there's any daylight and have them search out every nook and cranny this land has. You take the 'copter yourself. Just find that horse and find him quick."

"Hey," Andy told him, "you're forgetting there's a little girl lost out there, too."

"No I'm not. She's the one who set fire to a million dollars worth of horseflesh and darned near succeeded in burning me out. I'm not forgetting her." Wilson looked out across the darkened prairie, and his eyes were as somber as the night. "But right now, I'm concerned with finding a damn good barrel horse that's running on the loose out there. We'll deal with the girl later."

"But she's scared," Andy said softly.

"She damn well better be."

"She didn't mean you no harm," Gabriel tried to explain.

"She broke into my stables and burned them to the ground," Wilson growled. "She's a thief, and she stole from the wrong man this time. It's gonna cost somebody a bundle."

Andy's gaze moved with irritation from Wilson to Gabriel. She had had enough of both men and their selfish, self-righteous ways.

"The fire is tragic," she said, the patience gone from her voice. "And I'm sorry that it happened. But it wouldn't have happened at all if both of you had kept your stubborn, greedy hands off a horse that didn't belong to either one of you."

High upon a distant hill, beside a juniper tree, Barbara looked down at the charred stalls, ominous with the flashing red lights of the fire truck flickering across them. The tears had dried on her face. There was no reason to cry anymore. Barbara was drained, emotionless, a fugitive with no place to turn.

She glanced over her shoulder and stared at the prairie, hidden by the thickness of the night. It beckoned to her, a great unknown that quickened her pulse, yet frightened her as well. It would hide her. It would shelter her. Still, she hesitated, confused by what she knew she ought to do and what she had to do.

Barbara could give herself up, but she would lose Rebel, and he was all she had and all she wanted. Nobody would ever take him away from her again. Besides, she would probably go to jail if she turned herself in, and that

171

thought scared her more than being alone and on the run. At least she would be free. People couldn't hurt her anymore.

Gabriel had betrayed her.

Andy wouldn't want anything to do with a lawbreaker. Barbara was sure of it.

The sheriff would track her down. First though, she told herself, he would have to find her. And that wouldn't be easy.

Dejectedly, she turned Rebel slowly southward and together they moved quietly and forlornly into the darkness.

14

For days, the eyes of Caprock looked out across the bare prairie and saw only clusters of mesquite groves baked by the sun, scattered herds of whiteface cattle and an occasional tumbleweed whose journey had ended against the bottom strand of a barbwire fence. Turkey vultures scoured the countryside for calves or varmints too weak to survive the summer drought. Hawks rode the high currents of a southern wind, far above the helicopter that swept across the buffalo grass plains, searching for any trace that might have been left by the girl who had fled with her horse.

Fence riders were no longer content to merely check for breaks along those miles of weathered barbwire. They were more concerned with finding Rebel grazing somewhere out on the prairie and bringing him back home again. They held no grudge against Barbara

Atkins, figuring the fire had probably been an accident just like she had told Grady it was. Most even sympathized with her. And none blamed her for taking the big sorrel. They understood well the bond that develops between man and animal out in the vast stretches of West Texas where one sometimes cannot survive without the other. To most of them, a horse was family.

Warren P. Wilson, however, had offered a five thousand dollar reward for the return of the horse. No one could afford to turn his back on that kind of money, regardless of his personal feelings.

Time was running out on them all.

Saturday would be the final running of the West Texas Barrel Racing Championship Series. Sharon Wilson knew she had two chances to win. Her father could either find the one horse fast enough to carry her to victory, or he could make sure that Barbara Atkins did not show up at the arena to run against her. Sharon did not particularly care which option he chose, just as long as she was the one who wound up sitting tall and pretty in the winner's circle.

Wilson was tired and frustrated. He had owned Rebel. He had lost the big horse. Some people in town were beginning to laugh at him, and nobody laughed at Warren P. Wilson. Not for long anyway. His frustration had turned to anger.

He stormed into the office of J.T. Rodriguez without bothering to knock. The sheriff, working on his daily administrative reports, looked up and nodded.

"Morning," he said.

Wilson brushed all pleasantries aside. "I want Barbara Atkins arrested," he snapped.

Rodriguez leaned back in his imitation leather swivel chair and folded his arms. "I will, Mr. Wilson," he replied politely, "just as soon as we find her."

"You ought to be out there looking for her yourself."

The sheriff pulled out a file of complaints and arrest warrants, shuffled through them for a moment, then spread them out across the top of his desk.

"I'd like to go out and look for Barbara," Rodriguez answered. "I'd like to find her. Frankly, I'm worried about her. But Juan Gomez wanted to fight last night instead of going on home like he was supposed to. Homer Evans was rolled for three dollars and fourteen cents. Anson Finley's service station was burgled. And Joe Holland got mad at his wife again and said he was gonna shoot her if she threw him out, and you know old Joe's wife. She threw him out. You know, Mr. Wilson, I'm afraid we got a lot more going on in this town besides a pint-sized girl and a runaway horse."

Wilson leaned forward, propping his clenched fists on the desk. His black eyes glowered at the sheriff. His voice was that of a man who expected his every word to be obeyed without hesitation or argument.

"You better remember, sheriff," he said coldly, "that the county commissioners run this office, and I run the county commissioners. I can be real rough on you, and I will if I have to. I can make it easy or I can make it hard because I'm the man who controls your budget. I put you

175

into office. I can take you out. You do what I say or you better start stacking up stove wood because it's gonna be a long, cold winter."

Rodriguez looked away from the harsh stare that burned through him. He wiped the sweat away from his brow. "You shouldn't be worried, Mr. Wilson," he said. "Your daughter may not be riding the fastest horse in the barrel races come Saturday night. But then, it doesn't look like she'll have to run against him either. Diamond Cutter's a cinch to beat the rest of the horseflesh in this county."

"Maybe. Maybe not. That's a chance I don't want to have to take."

"We'll find Barbara, Mr. Wilson."

"Somebody's gonna find her, sheriff." Wilson walked briskly across the floor, paused at the door and turned back toward Rodriguez. "You better hope that it's you."

He slammed the door and was gone. The sheriff sighed, stacked the reports neatly, and reached for the keys to his patrol car. Some days his badge felt heavy, and this was one of them.

Wilson stood on the street corner and watched Rodriguez drive away as the warm winds cooled the anger that seethed deep inside of him. The streets around him were virtually empty, but a frantic sense of urgency was surging through his viens. He glanced out toward a vast stretch of prairie that hid the horse his daughter wanted so badly, the horse he must find and find quickly. Wilson knew he needed all the help he could get, and he needed it as fast as he could get it.

He straightened his jacket, adjusted his hat, and walked across the street and into the dimly-lit downtown domino parlor. Someone was always there, day or night. Wilson wanted every eye in Caprock out searching for Rebel, and he certainly didn't mind paying for it.

Without breaking stride, he headed toward the far corner table where Luke and Harmon had teamed up against two of their ranch hands. His footsteps on the old plank floor were the most audible sounds in the parlor. A naked light bulb above Wilson's head swung gently back and forth, causing splintered shadows to dance oddly on the wall.

Wilson stood for a moment beside the table, waiting to be recognized. No one bothered to look his way. He cleared his throat and Luke, frowning, leaned back in his chair and spoke without ever looking up from the dominoes he had lined up in front of him.

"What brings you in here, Mr. Wilson?" he drawled. "Am I late on my tractor payments again?"

Wilson forced a smile. "No, Luke," he answered. "In fact, I believe that tractor's just about paid for if I remember correctly."

"Probably. It's broke down now and never did run too good anyhow."

Luke downed the double five. Wilson shifted his weight from one foot to the other.

"I want to talk to you gentlemen about a horse," he said.

"I sold mine when I bought my pickup," Luke retorted.

"I got a little old mule," Harmon said, grinning

177

through his gray whiskers. "He ain't too fast, but he don't eat much, and he keeps the coyotes away from my calves."

Wilson's smile turned sour. Irritation pricked at his skin like a heat rash. Not even the ceiling fan above could dry the sweat that beaded his face.

"You know doggone well which horse I'm talking about," Wilson snapped, losing his patience. "Rebel has been stolen and I want him back. And I want him back before Saturday. Neither one of you is doing me any good sitting here and wasting time when you ought to be out there looking for the horse. I'm offering a five thousand dollar reward. But for you boys, I'll throw in another thousand if you find him. Now that's a better deal than dominoes any day."

"You already got half the county out looking," Harmon said. He played the ace - six and made a dime. "What makes you think we can do you any good?"

"Nobody knows this county better than you and Luke," Wilson replied. "Your granddaddies settled it. Your daddies ranched it. Both of you grew up on it. You've ridden through canyons that most folks don't even know are out there. If anybody can find the horse, you can."

Luke leaned back in his chair and silently turned the dominoes face down in front of him. "The way I see it," he said, "the horse don't rightfully belong to you anyway, Mr. Wilson. Rebel belongs to the girl."

"I bought it."

"Who'd you buy it from?"

178

"Gabriel."

Harmon laughed. "Gabriel would sell you Niagara Falls, and he don't own that either."

"It's legal," Wilson retorted.

"That don't necessarily make it right." Luke's voice was as coarse as gravel.

You know what I'm offering," Wilson said with a sigh. "Five grand, maybe more if you bring me the horse before Saturday. That's more money than most of you have ever seen at one time before. Think about it. You can find me at the ranch."

Wilson turned and walked quickly across the wooden floor, his jaws tight, his eyes cold. He wanted to see men jump when he spoke, and it troubled him when these ornery, independent old cowboys refused to take him seriously. As he stepped outside of the domino parlor, Wilson found himself face-to-face with Gabriel. The old man looked tired and drained. The cantankerous spirit that once burned brightly in his eyes had died out.

Gabriel grabbed Wilson's arm to stop him. "I knew I'd find you if I kept looking long enough," he said. "Wilson, let's me an' you make another deal for that horse. Sell him back to me and maybe we can get Barbara back before she gets hurt out there."

A look of disdain crossed the rancher's face. "Gabe," he snapped, "get it through your thick skull once and for all. Rebel belongs to Sharon and she aims to win the championship on that horse. You just make sure I get him back before the race."

"I shouldn't have sold him to you in the first place."

"But you did." The sun went behind a cloud, and the shadow passed slowly across the two men. "And it's final." There was no hint of compromise in Wilson's eyes. "You can forget about buying him back," he said. "You don't have anything I want."

Gabriel watched Wilson walk away. He leaned heavily against the doorway for support. The heat was stifling, and the old man had trouble breathing. He was as wilted as an okra patch beneath an unmerciful August sun.

Gabriel stepped inside the cool, darkened interior of the domino parlor and stood for a moment as the ceiling fan above him dried the sweat that had gathered around the ragged edges of his beard. Gabriel has never felt quite so alone in his entire life. What he needed, he told himself, were friends who would stand up for him.

He ambled toward the table at the far corner of the building, past the blue and yellow blinking lights of a jukebox that either played Hank Williams songs or didn't play anything at all. He and Luke had chased down a lot of maverick calves together. Gabriel had nursed Harmon's prize bull back to health in the days when the two-bit cattleman didn't have a tin can to spit in or a window to throw it out of. They would understand his plight. They would sympathize with him. They had all plowed a lot of new ground behind the same ornery old mule. Sometimes that made men closer than brothers.

"Who's winning?" Gabriel asked loudly, smiling, trying not to show the pain that throbbed angrily within him.

"Nobody." Luke frowned and, one by one, the four

men turned their dominoes face down on the table. "I'm afraid the game's over," he said.

"We don't mind playing with drunks, Gabriel," Harmon explained quietly. "And we ain't got nothing against playing with lepers, snakes, and hogs in a mud wallow..."

He paused and Luke finished the sentence for him. "But, Gabriel," he said, "you sold that little girl's horse. There are some things we can tolerate and some we can't. What you did is downright sinful. The law may give you the right to sell Rebel and steal Barbara's championship right out from under her, but we don't. You can play dominoes anywhere you want to, but you're gonna have to look somewhere else to find a partner."

"I didn't come here to play dominoes, Luke," Gabriel said, almost apologetically. "I came here to see if you would rent me one of your horses."

"I didn't think you rode horses anymore."

"Mostly I don't." Gabriel scratched his chin and shrugged. "Sometimes I have to."

"I got the old bay you can take," Luke said, nonchalantly shuffling the dominoes. "He's gentle enough. You can keep him as long as you need to, Gabe." He paused, then added caustically, "Just make sure you don't sell him before you get him back home again."

Gabriel nodded, too tired to argue or even defend himself anymore. He left the domino parlor without another word and headed across the street, toward the courthouse where Andy Beck's office was located. The old man limped down a long basement corridor, glanced

181

at her name on the door and walked in without bothering to knock.

Andy ignored him. She was staring at the county map that had been taped to her north wall, using a pencil to trace off the myriad farm and dirt roads that crisscrossed their way through the prairie grasses. Some went nowhere. Some, it seemed, just twisted through the brakes and canyons forever, following old cow and goat trails, hooking onto other roadways that appeared to have no end to them. Frustrated, Andy ripped the map off the wall and was rolling it up when she acknowledged that Gabriel was in the room with her.

She glared at him. "Well, Gabriel," she said, "have you spent your Judas money yet?"

"No, ma'am." He removed his hat politely and stuck his cigar back into his pocket. "I was comin' to ask you for a favor."

Andy eyed him suspiciously. "That's hard to believe," she answered.

"I'd like to borrow that horse trailer of yours."

"Why?"

"Well, I talked Luke outta one of his horses. But I gotta haul it plumb to the other side of the county if I have any chance at all of findin' Barbara."

"Do you know where she is?" Andy's face brightened.

"Maybe."

Andy dropped the map on her desk and began rolling up the sleeves of her blue-checked shirt. "Sure, you can borrow my trailer," she said, "but I go with it."

"I don't want your help, Miss Andy, just your trailer."

Andy folded her arms obstinately. "I'm going with you," she told him bluntly, "and there's no arguing about it."

"The country's rough," Gabriel said, making one last feeble effort to change her mind. "It ain't fit for a lady."

Andy smiled. "Why, thank you, Gabriel," she replied. "That's the nicest thing you've ever said about me."

She took the old man's arm and ushered him out of the office. Within minutes, they were seated in his battered blue pickup truck, rumbling toward the rodeo arena where Andy kept her trailer. Both windows were rolled down, and a hot wind blistered their faces.

"You surprise me, Gabe," Andy said, breaking the silence. "I didn't think you cared enough about Barbara to go after her."

"She belongs to me." The old man stared straight ahead down the highway. "Besides, I'm livin' on her place."

Andy frowned and crinkled her eyebrows in disbelief. "That place doesn't belong to Barbara."

"It does now." Gaberial's words were barely audible, caught, then brushed aside by the wind. "Barbara was dependin' on me, an' I didn't have nothin' to give her but my land. It ain't worth much, I guess. But it's all I had. Wilson wanted the horse and he held the deed to my little ranch, so we traded. An' he threw in a little money to boot. I had him put the land in Barbara's name, an' nobody can ever take it away from her. She owns the place now. I'm just the caretaker."

"Does Barbara know that?"

"I tried to tell her. I just never did figure out a very good way to do it."

Andy leaned her head back against the seat as Gabriel turned into the rodeo grounds. The sun hung overhead at about two o'clock. She hoped the day wouldn't give out on them. She had no idea just how far Gabriel was planning to ride.

15

A worn pickup truck, hauling a weather-beaten horse trailer, cut through a dry creekbed and picked its way up the rocky slope of a cedarbrake hill. It ground to a halt at the rim of a small mesa and an aging cowboy climbed out of the cab and looked across the empty stretch of land. Dust clung to his face, and it settled about his boots, scarred from too many years in the same stirrups.

John Price, tall and gangly, had worked on the Wilson Ranch for the past forty-four years, digging postholes, cutting cattle, riding fence lines, painting barns, doing whatever was asked of him. But this was, he had sworn, the first time he had ever wasted so many days chasing the shadow of a big sorrel horse and the wisp of a girl who rode him. His partner, Jay Phillips. leaned against the hood of the pickup, a pair of binoculars pressed firmly against his eyes. He was younger, intent on tracking

185

down the prey, constantly daydreaming about the reward and how he would spend it.

"She's gotta be out here somewhere," he said.

"There's just too many dadgummed places to hide out in these brakes," John told him.

"For five thousand dollars, I'll check 'em all out."

The aging cowboy grinned. "You may not have time to," he said. "It's already Friday. You got one day left, Jay, then it's back to counting, and culling cattle again."

"She can't stay hidden forever."

"She's done a pretty good job of it."

Jay's gaze swept past a herd of grazing white-faced cattle, focused for a moment on a cluster of mesquite trees, then eased along the banks of a creek, stopping suddenly as he made out the slender form of a young girl kneeling beside a trickle of spring water that poured out of a crease in the limestone. Behind her, as stately and as motionless as a stone statue, stood the big sorrel.

Jay grinned. "We've found her," he said quietly. "I hope Wilson pays in cash."

"Where do you see her?"

"Down by the creek. Let's go."

As John slipped back into the pickup truck, he looked at Jay and said, "I hope you're not planning on sneaking up on her out in this country."

"Nope." Jay's grin was broader. "I'm gonna run her until she's too tired to run, then me and that horse is going to the bank together."

At the base of the foothills, Barbara leaned over the small pool and saw the cracked reflection of her face in

186

the water. Her eyes were swollen, her pigtails unbraided, hair hanging limply on her thin shoulders. For three nights, there had been virtually no sleep at all, just restless hours of hunger, worry and indecision.

Barbara had grown weary of running, but she was too stubborn to give herself up. She was lonely, but free. More importantly, at least to her, she and Rebel were together again. Deep inside, even though Barbara refused to admit it to herself, she knew that her freedom could not last forever.

From her hiding place in the northern end of a box canyon, she had watched the helicopter as it swept low across the hilltops. And at times, Barbara had heard the faraway voices of the cowboys who patrolled the cedar brakes.

The country was big and sometimes seemed to stretch on for an eternity, wedged tightly against the blue of a western sky. Warren Wilson was a relentless man, she knew. His pride was at stake. So was his reputation. He would never stop looking until he found her. Barbara could run, but somewhere out on the prairie, the trap must slowly be closing in around her.

She splashed a handful of cold spring water against her face, washing away the dust and the grit that had collected there. Her hands shook, though not from fright, and her legs felt weak. Since her escape, Barbara had subsisted on mesquite beans and the moist meat of the prickly pear cactus that grew wild in the flats. It had kept her alive, but it wouldn't be able to keep her going much longer. She was kneeling again beside the spring for one last drink of water when she heard the unmistakable whine of a truck's engine, a ragged, unsettling noise that disturbed the silent world around her.

The pickup topped the hill with a frenzied roar, its tires chewing up dirt and spitting it out in all directions, grinding its way across the eroded crevices and cactus that blocked its path, sliding down the gentle slope as its wheels lost traction in the loose rocks. Barbara scrambled to her feet as the truck bore down upon her in a whirlwind of caliche dust and smoke, close enough for the smell of burning rubber to irritate her nostrils.

Rebel pranced nervously on the prairie floor.

In an instant, Barbara grabbed his mane and swung herself onto his back. The big sorrel bolted in a dead run back into the rock-strewn seam of a lost canyon.

The pickup churned across the narrow creek as John Price quick shifted it into a lower gear and cut sharply past the juniper that, for a moment, had obstructed his view of the fleeing horse.

Rebel was racing on flat ground now, picking up speed with every powerful stride, as free and easy as the wind and pushing just as hard. John Price knew the pickup would never be fast enough to catch the long-legged stallion. Then again, the truck would still be running long after the horse had dropped.

The cowboy grinned, and his partner grabbed the dash with both hands and hung on. All he had to do was keep Rebel in sight, dodge a few trees, jump a creek or two, and wait until the big sorrel broke and collapsed.

Over her shoulder, Barbara saw the truck slide

sideways as John Price fought the steering wheel. The trailer slammed into a boulder, bouncing off as the pickup gunned forward, threading its way through the mesquites, its engine groaning and grumbling and threatening to burst apart at any minute. The cowboys were losing ground, but Barbara could not shake them. They kept trailing her the way a pack of hungry coyotes follow a frightened calf. She bent low and buried her face in Rebel's wind-blown mane, holding on tightly as she ran the toughest race of her life over terrain so harsh that only the horned toads and rattlesnakes could survive it.

Barbara turned her horse into the sun, pushing him on up the hill, listening as the stuttering whine of the engine faded behind her. Only a little further to go, she thought. Only a few more yards. It wouldn't be much longer now and she would have the prairie to herself again. Through blurred eyes, Barbara could make out the lone juniper that loomed crookedly on the summit above her. Rebel dug his hooves into the dirt and strained forward, fighting his way to the top, carrying his mistress steadily onward toward the freedom she would find beyond the far side of the cactus rim. The big sorrel, his neck white with lather, surged across the crest of the hill, then stumbled into a ravine that rain and wind had chiseled into the sun-blistered face of the high country. He went down to his knees, struggling to recover his balance, screaming in defiance as he tried frantically to regain his footing in the crusty earth.

Barbara pitched forward and rolled across the ground as limp as a rag doll. She lay motionless, unconscious, as the sputtering sound of the pickup inched up the hillside. A long-eared jackrabbit leaped out of the brambles. A chaparral flashed into the sunlight and was gone. The throbbing noise of the truck jarred Barbara awake. She shook her head to chase away the cobwebs that had collected there. She wiped the dust from her freckled face, and it smeared the blood that dripped from a cut above her left eye.

She looked first for Rebel.

He stood quivering, silhouetted against the sky, his eyes full of fire, ready to go as soon as Barbara called on him to run again. The big stallion neighed softly. Barbara slowly stood, winced as a sharp pain tore through her ankle, and limped toward him.

"They don't have us yet," she said grimly.

The pickup was rapidly eating up the distance though, closing in from behind. Every second counted and Barbara knew that time was against her. But then, she guessed, it always had been.

The truck spun onto the hilltop as she mounted, so near she could almost feel the heat radiating out from beneath the hood.

Barbara mounted and Rebel bolted into a clump of mesquite atop the mesa. The truck, too, knifed its way through the gnarled limbs, breaking those that grew too low and too close to the heavy duty bumper. For John Price, the girl was almost within his reach, and he realized he might never get this close again. He could already feel the five thousand dollars in his hip pocket as he jammed the accelerator to the floorboard, slinging the horse

190

trailer against the trees, ripping it from the old, rusted hitch, and leaving it bent and busted, tumbling down into the pit of the ravine.

Barbara was riding hard over the western edge of the brakes when the truck, spinning out of control, lurched past the rim and dropped suddenly down the sheer rock face of the hilltop. It bounced once, then twice, as tires blew and the frame snapped. The pickup was thrown into the brown, tepid waters of a stock pond, scattering whiteface cattle and coming to rest, at last, in silence beneath the broad, black wings of the turkey vultures that soared in the hot air currents that rose up from the prairie. The truck settled axle-deep in the mud. The engine belched once, then quit for good. By the time John Price and Jay Phillips had waded ashore, Barbara and the big sorrel were out of sight.

In anger and frustration, neither cowboy spoke as they trudged through the hills, following an old, well-worn cow trail that finally led them out of the back country and on to the edge of the Caprock highway.

The heat had sapped them and the rocks hurt their feet. They weren't used to walking. Cowboys, for years, had sworn, "If I can't do it horseback, then I won't do the job." Most eventually traded their horses for pickup trucks, but still they rode everywhere they went. John Price didn't like walking, particularly during the sun-baked days of summer. There were no clouds to bring relief. The earth itself was a furnace, and he could feel the temperature rising off the ground like a nagging fever. John's legs ached, his back was stiff, his shirt was soaked with sweat. He and Jay paused and stared down that long, narrow ribbon of concrete that wound through the valley. In the distance, they saw the dim outline of a Chevy pickup headed their way.

Jay Phillips limped out into the middle of the highway and began frantically waving his arms as the truck slowed to a stop. He hurried around to the driver's side as Andy Beck, frowning, rolled down her window.

"Miss, you gotta take us back to town," the cowboy blurted out. "It's real important."

"I'm not going that way."

"We gotta find the sheriff," John Price said, leaning against the truck. "We don't have any time to waste."

"Why?" Andy eyed them suspiciously.

"It was your grandbaby, Gabe," John said. "We found her and we danged near had her, too."

Gabriel spoke up for the first time. "Is she all right?"

"She's a heckuva lot better off than we are." Disappointment crept into John's voice. "I had that five grand so close to me I could almost smell it and dang near had it all spent."

Jay turned and pointed westward. "We must've chased her from one end of those hills to the other," he said.

"Where did you last see her?" Andy wanted to know.

"Just the other side of Sawtooth Mountain, back where the Barber gang holed up so long the bloodhounds went lame."

"Which direction was she going?"

"West." It was Gabriel who answered. A sly smile creased his grizzled face.

"You betcha," John replied. "She was headed right into the sun, running flat out and wide open. We had her cornered, and there was no way she was gonna get away from us."

"Till we lost the trailer," Jay added.

"And had a blowout on the right front tire."

"And hit old man Taylor's stock pond."

John Price shook his head sadly. "I thought that old pickup would run forever," he said softly. "But the sucker sank like a potbellied rock."

Andy drove away and left the two cowboys stranded, standing in their own misery beside the scorched highway. They were on their way to town. She wasn't. They were looking for the sheriff. All she wanted to find was a little thirteen-year-old girl who had already spent too many days alone and on the run in a broad and unforgiving land.

Andy turned to Gabriel, curiosity in her eyes. "How did you know which way Barbara was going?"

"Just a hunch."

"It must have been a good one."

"Yeah." Gabriel grinned as he rolled his cigar from one side of his mouth to the other. "It looks like Barbara may have paid attention to old Yellow Feather after all."

Andy raised an eyebrow. "I don't understand," she said.

"You will," the old man replied. "Barbara's a smart little girl. She hears a lot and don't forget nothin'. She's stubborn, got a mind of her own, and is tough as a boot."

"She sounds a lot like you," Andy said smiling.

193

"She's even more like her mama."

Andy pulled the pickup to a stop beside Juanita Madrone's barn. She and Gabriel quickly saddled their horses, mounted, and headed toward the purple afternoon haze that had settled down around the rugged summit of Sawtooth Mountain. It was about three hours before sundown, but the heat had not lost its unrelenting grip on the prairie.

Andy stood in her stirrups and looked out across the bitter terrain. "I'm not surprised that no one has found Barbara," she said. "This is good country to hide in."

Gabriel nodded. "I came in here lookin' for a stray calf one year," he told her. "I found it the day before it died."

"What killed it?"

"Old age."

Andy laughed, but her eyes continued to probe the wild, unruly landscape that stretched out before her, searching for any trace, no matter how slight, that Barbara and the big sorrel might have left behind. The land lay flat and unbroken, tracked only by varmints, as jackrabbits played hide and seek with the coyotes that wandered there. Andy raised a hand to shield her face from the sun, and a lazy little breeze ruffled her hair.

"I saw you talking with Wilson earlier today," she said.

The old man nodded. "He wants that dadgummed horse back, and he don't care what it costs him."

"Is that why you're really out here?" Andy asked. "Did you promise to find Rebel for him. Is that part of your deal? How much is he going to pay you this time?"

Gabriel looked hurt, and the pain was tempered with

anger. "Lady," he snapped, "I haven't been on a horse in seventeen years. I doctor 'em, but I don't ride 'em. I ain't had nothin' to eat since sundown yesterday, an' I'm gettin' blisters so long they're growin' to the seat of my britches. So if you think I'm out here for any other reason than tryin' to help Barbara, then you got about as much sense as that stump over there."

"You let her down when you sold Rebel."

Gabriel shrugged. "I'm afraid that my generation just always believed a horse was a horse. Men used 'em to work with, not play with. They were tools, not pets." The old man sighed. "I guess me an' my kind just kind of got left behind with the times."

"Times do change," Andy said softly.

"Old men don't."

"You can try."

"I already have." Gabriel reined his horse to a stop and squatted as he looked at the alkali flats around him. "Change don't come easy," he admitted. "It never has. I don't guess it ever will."

"Are you sure you know where you're going?"

"Landmarks haven't changed at all since me an' Miriam used to come back in here when she was a little girl." Gabriel grinned as the memories came back to him. "Just beyond that ridge is a little valley," he said. "There's a creek in the bottom of it, an' me an' Miriam used to camp alongside that creek. I taught her to ride in this valley. It was on an old swayback mule named Matilda. The mule wasn't much to ride, but she could flat plow a good garden."

At the rim of the canyon, Gabriel and Andy dismounted and led their horses single file down a narrow, switchback trail that wound its way precariously toward the creek. The old man was limping, his shoulders slumped as the simmering heat began to drain him and take its toll. Even so, Gabriel was like an old war horse who would not give up. He and the land had a lot in common. They were sometimes tenacious, sometimes gentle, and always unpredictable. Gabriel lost his footing, but grabbed the sharp edge of a boulder to regain his balance, pausing a moment to catch his breath. Andy had been frustrated by the cantankerous old man for years and often angered by him. She seldom trusted him and never really felt comfortable with him. Now she had to admit a grudging admiration.

"You want to stop and rest a minute?" she asked.

Gabriel shook his head. "If I let these old knees tighten up now," he replied, "I may as well throw 'em away. Besides, I ain't hurtin' near as bad as that little girl."

"I hope she's all right."

"That horse'll take care of her if Barbara lets him." Gabriel led his mount off the slope of the canyon and into the gently rolling midsection of the valley. "He can find a little food in places where you might think there ain't nothing to eat. And he can smell water miles away."

Andy looked surprised. "You sound like you've got a lot of faith in that horse," she said.

"Animals never let you down like people do."

Andy climbed back into the saddle and removed her right boot, shaking out a fistful of dust, then gingerly picking out stray cactus thorns that had collected in the legs of her jeans. She grimaced. "Not even the devil himself would want this country," she said.

"It's good land," Gabriel argued.

"It's dry and rocky and dusty and not fit for anything but snakes and horned lizards."

"They gotta live someplace."

"I don't like them living with me."

Gabriel grinned. "They were here first," he said. "And they'll be here long after we're just part of the dust."

He rode off toward the western foothills of Sawtooth Mountain. Andy called after him, "Are you positive you know where you're going?"

"I know where I'm going," he yelled back over his shoulder. "I only hope Barbara's there."

The sun was hanging low and an uneasy wind had chased the heat from the valley by the time Gabriel and Andy galloped out of the long shadows and to the base of a waterfall that tumbled like a slender thread out of the mountain.

Gabriel dismounted and tied his horse to a juniper growing out of a crack in the rocks, slowly climbing back through a clump of thorned underbrush that for decades had hidden the dry-wall cavern where Chief Yellow Feather found refuge while the Texas Rangers dogged his tracks. Andy followed him through the veil of cascading water, stepping silently into a great, chilled room that had been carved out of the western slope of Sawtooth. They heard Rebel neigh softly, and his hoofsteps echoed throughout the cave.

"Hello, boy," Andy said, and there was relief in her voice. "I'm sure glad to see you. Now where's Barbara?"

She blinked, and gradually her eyes became accustomed to the darkness. A dim glow, sunlight filtering through the waterfall, pervaded the stone room. Behind the big sorrel, Andy saw Barbara sleeping on a rock ledge, wrapped in an old, frayed saddle blanket.

Andy knelt beside the girl and gently touched her shoulder. Barbara awoke with a start, her eyes wide with fright as she realized that she was no longer alone. All she could make out was the shadows of two figures hovering above her. Barbara slung the blanket away and came off the ledge kicking and scratching, clawing her way toward the freedom that kept eluding her.

Andy gabbed the girl and held her tightly. "It's all right," she whispered.

"Let me go!" Barbara yelled, alarmed.

"We're here to help you, Barb." Andy's voice was calm, soothing. "You can stop running now. You don't have to hide any longer."

Barbara looked past Andy, and her glare cut deeply into Gabriel's wrinkled face.

"He's not here to help me," she spit out bitterly. "He's here to get Rebel and take him away from me again."

"No, Barb." Andy felt Barbara relax, and she loosened her grip on the girl's frail shoulders. "Gabriel's here to take you home, and that's where you belong."

"I can't go back." Barbara's voice broke. "They're gonna put me in jail if I go back."

"They can't arrest you for runnin' away with your own

198

horse," Gabriel told her. "He's yours, and I didn't have any right to sell him. I did it, an' I'm sorry. I don't know how just yet, but I'm gonna get Rebel back for you. You can bank on it."

Barbara smiled. Andy brushed the streaks of dirt and blood from her cheeks.

"What happened to you, Barb?"

"I fell."

"Does it hurt?"

"Not anymore."

Gabriel sat down beside his granddaughter and took her hand in his. "You know, Barb," he said, "I once had an old hound dog, he wasn't purebred or nothin' an' he never caught a jackrabbit in his life, but he was a good old dog. I took off to Colorado one summer an' left him sittin' by the front door steps waitin' on me. I got to havin' a high old time, an' it was two months before I came on home again. When I got back, he was gone. I swore then I'd never be so unkind and so stupid as to hurt and lose anything important to me again." He paused, then added, "But it looks like I did."

"Rebel?"

"The girl that rides him so good."

"Me?"

Gabriel nodded, and Barbara's eyes brightened.

"I couldn't believe you sold Rebel. I love him so much."

"Yeah." Gabriel shrugged. "An' till you came along, I had just kind of forgotten what that was all about."

Barbara rested her head on the old man's shoulder as he put his arm around her. She felt more at peace with

199

herself than she had for a long time.

"I always wanted a granddaddy," Barbara said wistfully. "I really did, especially at Christmas and on Valentine's Day. I always made something for you, but you never came to get it. You never came to see me at all. Why didn't you come?"

"Well, I would have, girl," the old man blustered, "but my mule died. Then my plow broke. An' the chickens got in the okra patch one year. An'...." Gabriel sighed. He knew he had been lying to himself for years. There was no reason to lie to the little girl. "I never came around because you reminded me so much of your mama," he said finally. "I missed her so much, an' I didn't want nothin' remindin' me I didn't have her anymore."

"I could have taken her place," Barbara whispered.

"I wished I'd a let you." Gabriel scratched his chin. There was sadness etched in his eyes. "I've done a lot of fool things in my life —"

"That's just the price you pay for living so long," Andy interrupted him. "Come on, Gabe, let's take Barbara back home so she can sleep in her own bed for a change."

"What about Rebel?" the girl asked cautiously.

"Right now, he still belongs to Mr. Wilson," Andy told her.

"Do I have to give him back?"

"For the time being."

"Then I'm not going." There was determination in her voice and in her eyes. "Not unless I ride Rebel tomorrow night. Maybe he does belong to Mr. Wilson. Maybe they'll put me in jail for running off with him. But daddy bought Rebel so we could win that championship together, and I'm gonna make sure that Rebel has the chance to be a champion."

"It's too much of a risk," Andy argued.

"I'll take it." Barbara wasn't budging from her decision.

"You could get hurt."

A slow grin spread across the girl's face. "I can take care of myself," she said.

Gabriel nodded. "You've already proven that," he admitted. "But you winnin' that championship on another man's horse ain't exactly what they'd call legal."

"We may not get the trophy," Barbara replied. "But trophies don't matter. In our hearts, we'll always know we won. Nobody can ever take that away from us."

Gabriel glanced at Andy. He knew she was torn between duty and emotion.

At last she turned to Barbara and told her, "When I was fifteen, I fell and cut my leg. It took sixteen stitches to sew it up. But I was a tough little girl and wanted to go ahead and swim in the junior high district meet. My father was a very wise and understanding man."

"Did he let you swim?"

"No," Andy sighed, "and I never forgave him."

"Then I can ride tomorrow night?"

Andy stood and walked toward the front of the cave. "I shouldn't let you," she said, "but I certainly won't stand in your way."

Barbara's laughter was a squeal.

"Well, if you're gonna ride," Gabriel said, "let's make

sure it's a dadgummed good one."

Outside, the sky had turned from red to a deep purple, and the last rays of a lingering sunset were retreating from the length and the breadth of the prairie.

16

The stores closed early that Saturday afternoon in downtown Caprock. By four o'clock the square was virtually empty, and almost everyone had already begun making the two mile trek out to the fairgrounds for the final running of the Barrel Racing Championship.

It was a special day, one that had all the trappings of a carnival sideshow. And long before sundown, the dusty parking lot was jammed with pickup trucks, horse trailers and vendors selling foot-long hotdogs, steaming off the grill, smothered with chili, cheese, and onions. Children plastered their faces with cotton candy. Members of the high school band filed into their seats just below the announcer's stand, and someone with a trumpet haphazardly blew *CHARGE* as a runaway horse bolted wildly across the arena floor.

Back behind the grandstand, girls proudly paraded

their mounts, full of fear, hope and nervous energy that would not disappear until the ride had ended. They had waited so long for this night. It would be over so quickly. They wanted to savor every minute of it. Yet there was an awkward tension among them, one they had never experienced before.

Someone was missing.

Their laughter was tempered by their concern for Barbara. She should be there, they knew. She should be riding for the championship trophy and saddle. By all rights, it belonged to her anyway. Rebel was undefeated. No one had even come close to beating the big sorrel.

Where was Barbara?

What had happened to her and Rebel?

The whole county, it seemed, had been out scouring the countryside for a week, and no one had even found a trace of Barbara, although two old cowboys were swearing they had almost run her down. But they had always had a bad habit of stretching the truth. Most didn't know whether to believe them or not.

Andy Beck, the barrel racers noticed, was in a better mood than usual, but no one knew why. She was probably just trying to make them all feel better, patiently talking with each girl, giving them last-minute instructions, along with a hug and a smile and a word or two of encouragement. "Don't be obsessed with winning," she kept telling them. "Winning's not everything. And don't be upset with losing. There's always another year, another chance. Just do the best that you can do and be glad you had the opportunity to ride." The girls nodded, but few were listening. They were lost in their own thoughts, worries, and dreams.

Sharon Wilson stood apart, the sequins on her blouse flashing reds and golds, lit by the last rays of the afternoon sun. Her long ebony hair fell down around her shoulders, and her face was flushed with frustration as she watched Diamond Cutter being unloaded from his trailer. Tonight was the night she had expected to ride Rebel. Now he was gone, and her pride was hurt.

"Don't worry, sweetheart," her father said as he handed her the reins. "You can't lose."

"What makes you say that?"

"There's no one here who can beat you."

"Rebel could."

"Rebel's not here." Wilson grinned and hugged his daughter. "I'll guarantee you that Diamond Cutter is the fastest horse in the arena tonight."

"He'd better be."

Sharon angrily spun around and walked away, leading the big black horse behind her. The silver inlay glistened in the saddle, and Diamond Cutter's ears perked up as he heard the band strike up John Phillip Sousa's marching music in the arena. But he shied away from the leather quirt that Sharon was swinging at her side, flinching as she occasionally slapped it sharply against the tops of her ostrich skin boots.

Andy shuffled through the entry forms, straightened them again, and headed toward the announcer's table. Everyone had been accounted for. Everyone, that is, except Barbara. And Barbara, Andy knew, was on her way, determined to make the ride of her life. She could no longer win the championship, not officially anyway. She would be mounted on somebody else's horse. But pride was at stake. Barbara had vowed to end the season as she had begun it, riding on the back of a winner.

Andy paused at the gate and glanced back over her shoulder. Gabriel sat perched atop a wagon load of hay, his eyes fixed upon the hills as the night slowly came and hid them behind a curtain of darkness. The old man had chewed his cigar down to a stub. The collar of his shirt was soaked with sweat. The heat still lingered oppressively upon the prairie.

Around him, Gabriel saw that everyone was in place, mingling nonchalantly on the outskirts of the crowd, out of the way and waiting for the sun to drop beyond the mesquites. Perhaps they wouldn't be needed, but Gabriel was taking no chances. He looked at his gold pocketwatch and smiled. It wouldn't be long now.

Behind him, he heard the familiar gravel voice of Red Henke:

Good evenin', ladies and gentlemen, and welcome to the championship runnin' of West Texas Barrel Racing, where we'll be crowning a brand new girl's champion tonight. And let's get it all started with little Miss Kathy Turner who is currently in tenth place.

As Kathy charged toward the first barrel, Andy slipped past Warren P. Wilson's box seat and hurried toward the scorer's table. The rancher frowned as he saw her file a new entry sheet, and his eyes followed her as she ran up the steps to Red Henke's booth. Wilson had never seen

206

Andy in that much of a rush before, and it bothered him.

Henke boomed, *That's a fine time of eighteen point four for Kathy. Betty Sullivan, you're up next.*

He looked up as Andy handed him a new entry list.

"There's been a change," she said.

Henke quickly scanned the list and whistled softly as he came to Barbara's name.

"You sure Barbara's gonna be ridin'?" he asked.

Andy nodded gravely. "She'll be here," she said, then lowered her voice to a whisper. "But I'd appreciate your not mentioning it until she comes through the gate."

Henke grinned. "Whatever you want sounds good to me."

"Thanks."

Henke turned to his microphone.

Let's give Betty a big hand," he said. *"She had a good time, a fast seventeen point two. But I'm afraid that knockin' down that second barrel's gonna cost her ten seconds and drop her a notch behind Kathy Turner in the final standings.*

Wilson ambled up to the scorer's table and picked up the entry list. "When is Sharon up?" he asked.

"She drew the seventh position."

Wilson ignored him. His only concern was the entry sheet that Andy Beck had slipped in at the last minute, and anger filled his eyes when he saw the name of Barbara Atkins pencilled in at the bottom of the paper. Wilson slowly crumpled the form, dropped it to the ground, and kicked it as he walked quickly away.

Below him, Kimberly Hampton atop Old Slewfoot was

rounding the final barrel and heading for home. The people were on their feet screaming and Wilson pushed his way through them, turning a deaf ear to the applause and the roll of drums that grew louder as the girl raced past the finish line. He climbed across the railing and leaped to the arena floor, searching in the crowd for Grady.

He had been betrayed, Wilson told himself. He had never trusted Gabriel. Now it looked like Andy Beck had also chosen to blatantly defy him, and that was a mistake she would regret for a long time.

Grady, leaning his tall, lanky frame against the horse trailer, saw his boss man approaching. He could tell by the way Wilson was moving that trouble was brewing. Grady could handle blizzards, droughts, prairie fires, even hoof-and-mouth disease in cattle, but didn't like finding himself caught up in the middle of a family problem. Grady was at the mercy of the man who paid her salary, and at the moment that man was more concerned with barrel racing than ranching.

"We got troubles," Wilson yelled.

The sun balanced itself on the horizon for a moment like a gold doubloon, then slipped out of sight.

"That Atkins girl is gonna be riding here tonight," Wilson continued as he reached Grady's side. "At least she thinks she is."

"It won't do her any good," Grady replied.

The cold, unforgiving look on Wilson's face stopped him. "If Sharon can't ride Rebel in the championships," the rancher snapped, "then I don't want that little thief riding him either."

Grady shrugged, glad for the darkness that had finally descended on the earth.

"Get some help," Wilson told him. "I don't care how many men it takes, but stop her. Make sure that that little girl never gets here."

Grady's voice was tired. "Don't you think we've caused Barbara enough grief?" he questioned.

"Stop her!"

Grady nodded. "You're still the boss," he said.

Out on the prairie, Barbara led Rebel down an arroyo and onto the crest of a bald-knob mesa. In the distance, she could see the yellowed lights clustered around the arena walls and could just hear the muffled roar of the crowd as it rolled randomly across the barren plains. She wondered who was running and how fast her time had been. She thought about Sharon. There was a bitter taste in her mouth. Sharon had it all, and still she wasn't satisfied.

The braids had fallen from Barbara's hair, and it blew gently against her face. The cool winds soothed the cuts above her eyes. She could feel her nerves becoming unraveled in the pit of her stomach. She was always nervous. But this was the first time she had been afraid. She didn't like the way fear had stuck in her throat. Barbara tried to swallow it, and Rebel nuzzled his head against her shoulder and whinnied softly. The girl sighed without a smile and climbed upon his back.

It was almost time now.

The big sorrel was dancing beneath her, ready and

eager to run.

Barbara wondered if she could make it to the arena without anyone seeing her. Gabriel had told her not to worry, that he would make sure she had a clear path to the gate. But what if something went wrong — what if someone stopped her? What if her ride was all in vain? Barbara shook the doubts from her mind, placed her faith in Gabriel B. Spencer, and turned toward Caprock.

The wait was over.

There would be no turning back now.

Barbara had one ride left. She promised herself that it would be an unforgettable one. The darkness raced past her as she flattened out atop the big sorrel, letting his long, powerful strides carry her ever closer to the fairgrounds.

On the western edge of the parking lot, Grady had directed two cowboys, John Price and Jay Phillips, to move their pickup trucks alongside the main entrance to the arena. He pointed toward the prairie and told them matter-of-factly, "If she's coming at all, she'll be coming out of those foothills."

"What are we supposed to do with her?" John asked.

"Just make sure she doesn't get to those barrels."

"We'll stop her."

Grady lowered his head and walked away. "Just don't hurt her," he said. "She's a little girl, and she's already been hurt enough."

Inside the arena, Henke was saying,

Miss Cynthia Anderson has broken that mystical seventeen second mark for the first time this year. She's

210

*got herself a sixteen point nine, and that's gonna win her a
dinner for two down at the downtown Hayes Cafe. And I
hope she takes me with her. Congratulations, Miss
Cynthia.*

Behind the arena, a smiling Sheriff Rodriguez had
reached up to help Cynthia dismount when Wilson
grabbed his shoulder.

"I've just learned that Barbara Atkins is coming to ride
my stolen horse here tonight," the rancher said,
discontent in his voice.

"Your grapevine's better than mine," Rodriguez
answered.

"I want her arrested."

"That's my job."

Wilson stepped closer to the sheriff, and he squeezed
his words through clenched teeth. "And I want her
arrested before she has a chance to run the barrels."

"I can put the cuffs on her," Rodriguez told him, his
patience growing thin. "But not until the horse stops."

"Don't worry," Wilson assured him. "I'll make sure the
horse stops running. You make sure the girl stops."

"You want them both, then."

The rancher nodded. "I want that horse in my barn,
and the girl in your jail."

He looked away as he heard Red Henke announce his
daughter's name.

*Up on Diamond Cutter, the pride of the Wilson
Ranches, all decked out in sequins and satin, is the lovely
Miss Sharon Wilson, currently in second place but
always a winner. Come a ridin' when you're ready, Miss*

211

Sharon.

By the time Wilson had sprinted to the arena, Sharon had cleared the first barrel of the cloverleaf pattern and was racing madly for the second one, her quirt slashing into the big horse's flanks with each stride he took. Diamond Cutter cut the second turn sharply, stormed around the third barrel, then bolted furiously for home, gaining speed each time the leather tip of the whip popped into his flesh.

Wilson was beaming as he heard Red Henke's voice boom out above the noise:

A sixteen point two. A new arena record. A great piece of ridin' for Miss Sharon Wilson.

The rancher smiled and felt a sense of vindication. He had been right. Sharon Wilson did have the fastest horse in the arena. Not even Rebel had come close to sixteen point two. He had said all along that Diamond Cutter was great horse-flesh, and now Sharon had proven it.

There are only two riders left tonight, Henke was saying to the crowd. *Can anyone catch Sharon Wilson?*

Wilson shook his head.

Nobody could, he knew. Not now. His daughter had the championship all wrapped up, and nobody else was even in the running. Wilson straightened his hat, and a broad grin spread across his face. Bloodlines will win out everytime, he told himself. Sharon had Wilson bloodlines.

Andy Beck glanced nervously at her watch, then walked quickly out of the arena as Wanda Parsons, riding the long-legged gray gelding that her granddaddy

212

had given her for Christmas, charged toward the first barrel. Gabriel was waiting for Andy beside a wagon load of hay, spitting the last leaves of his well-chewed cigar onto the ground.

"She ought to be coming by now," Andy said quietly. Yesterday, the decision to let Barbara ride had seemed so right. Now she wasn't sure. Her hands trembled as she stared out across the empty prairie. "Keep an eye out for her, Gabe. Don't let her get hurt."

"I ain't worried about Barbara none," the old man told her. "She's tough as boot leather." He nodded toward Grady, who was scanning the horizon with a pair of binoculars while the two ranch hands stood beside him, holding the reins of their horses. "But them guys are makin' me plumb nervous," he added.

"Do they know about Barbara?" Andy asked.

"Those are Wilson's men." Gabriel's voice was as dry as a desert wind. "An' I'd bet my bottom dollar that they ain't out lookin' for the big dipper."

"How do you reckon they found out?"

Gabriel shrugged. "I don't care how they found out," he said. "I just wonder what they plan on doin' when Barbara gets here."

He picked up a jack from the ground beside him and ambled as discreetly as possible toward Grady's truck.

In the distance, a lone, tiny rider, bending low in the saddle, raced out of the prairie, illuminated by the soft, gentle light of a new moon. The horse sprinted past the mesquites and veered suddenly toward the arena, barreling onto the parking lot itself. Grady and John

Price moved into the horse's path, frantically waving their hats.

On the microphone, Red Henke was saying,

A seventeen point four for Miss Wanda who was ridin' those barrels tonight like she owned 'em. A good ride on a good horse.

Henke paused dramatically, then continued.

And now, I'm told, we have ourselves a surprise entry. At least from what I hear she's on her way. Our current leader, ladies and gentlemen, little Miss Barbara Atkins on Rebel, comin' out of hidin', comin' on the run.

An excited roar from the stands showed Barbara and Rebel had some friends who were glad they were there.

The racing horse slowed and reared, his hooves pawing in the air, shadow boxing with the men who had blocked his way. Grady moved in without hesitation, jerking the reins loose, settling the nervous sorrel down. Price reached up and grabbed a wiry but frail arm, pulling the rider, kicking and fighting, out of the saddle as both fell in a tangled heap upon the ground. Grady knelt beside them and found himself staring into the grinning, impish face of Ricky Rodriguez.

Ricky winked.

Grady slammed his hat with disgust into the dirt.

"Gotcha!" Ricky said.

By the time Grady heard the galloping hoofbeats on the soft earth, they were already past him. He spun around and caught a glimpse of Rebel, far to the left, threading his way beneath the last row of cars, making his way steadily toward the arena gate. Barbara's eyes shone

214

in the moonlight, her jaws clenched in grim determination. There was only one chance to stop her.

And the voice of Red Henke filled the parking lot, *Miss Barbara, if you're out there somewhere. The arena's all yours.*

Jay Phillips was already mounted and riding hard across the dried grass in a mad dash to cut Barbara off and force her back out toward the highway. She swerved away. As the cowboy bolted toward her, Andy stood atop the wagon, kicked the rear gate open, and the loose hay bales came tumbling end over end around him. His horse shied and stumbled and Phillips pitched forward onto the caliche gravel, and he sat up spitting out a mouthful of dirt and hay and sun-parched straw.

Barbara swung wide, then reined Rebel back toward the arena, working her way carefully through the cars with the same delicate skill she used to run the barrels.

Grady leaped into his pickup truck and hit the ignition. The engine roared to a start.

He jammed his foot on the accelerator.

Nothing happened.

The motor whined and sang at a fever pitch.

And nothing happened.

The pickup rattled, and it shook, but it didn't go anywhere.

Outside, the back wheels were spinning wildly a good six inches off the ground, hoisted up by Gabriel's jack that had been strategically shoved beneath the rear axle. Grady killed the engine and slumped against the steering wheel as he watched the big sorrel, sweat glistening, his head held high, near the gate.

John Price took a last shot at stopping the girl. With tires squealing and rubber burning, he slid his pickup into the entrance to block her path. He was there only a moment or two before Gabriel's battered old blue truck came bouncing out of the darkness, ramming broadside into Price, driving him helplessly to the side, clearing the way for Barbara and Rebel to thunder into the stark glare of the arena spotlight.

Andy raised her arms in triumph.

Gabriel grinned like a mule grazing in a thicket patch.

And Warren P. Wilson angrily slammed his program against the wooden railing.

The roar of the expectant crowd began to swell as Rebel dug sharply around the first barrel and attacked the second.

Ricky was yelling.

The sheriff leaned forward on the scorer's table. He knew Wilson would make life miserable for him. He wondered why he was smiling.

The drum roll suddenly ceased. The tumult and the shouting died away. Even Henke had nothing to say.

The crowd was on its feet, watching in stunned silence, mesmerized, as the big sorrel stretched out around the final barrel and exploded toward the far end of the arena in a storm of dust and fury, powerful and strong, guided by a little girl who had looked defeat squarely in the eyes and refused to accept it. She was full of grit and bound for glory, driven on by a determination that would not be denied. She had lost so much, and now she was fighting back. It was a battle she could not win but would not lose. This moment, she knew, belonged to Rebel. It was his. He had earned it. The trophy might be given to someone else. Rules were rules. But everyone would know that Rebel had won, and, to Barbara, that was all that mattered.

Her father had showed faith in the colt. She had loved him. Together, for so long, they had been inseparable. Now their time together was growing short.

Rebel ran for her.

For no one else.

And Rebel had won.

Barbara knew it. In her heart, she felt it. The loudspeaker blaring across the plains had told her that Sharon had set an arena record with a sixteen point two. But Rebel had beaten it. There was no doubt in her mind.

The big sorrel had never run that hard before, nor that fast. There was, it seemed, always more speed coiled within him when Rebel needed it. It was as if he always knew what it took to win, and he always gave it.

For her.

For no one else.

Love could indeed make a difference.

They swept as one past the finish line, Barbara leaning against Rebel's thick neck, hanging onto his long, flowing mane, her eyes blurred by the wind and the tears that flowed as they dashed into the peaceful quiet of the night.

Henke's voice was restrained.

Sixteen flat! was all he said.

It was enough.

No one had ever run faster. Perhaps no one would ever

run that fast again, at least not on a subdued, restless summer night in Caprock, Texas.

Gabriel jumped off the plank fence and ran to find Barbara. John Price grabbed his arm and spun the old man around.

"You wrecked my truck deliberately," he accused.

Gabriel nodded. "I believe you're right," he said.

"I'll have your hide for this."

"Well then, you won't have much." Gabriel broke away from the man's grasp and turned his back on Price. He didn't have time to fool with angry cowboys. He and Price could settle their differences later. Right now, there was a little girl waiting all alone, and she needed him. She had needed him lots of times, but Gabriel had never been there before.

This time he wouldn't let her down.

He and Sheriff Rodriguez gently lifted Barbara from Rebel's back. She leaned, weak and exhausted, against them. Barbara's jeans had been torn by the cactus and her shirt hung loosely around her shoulders. Her face was swollen and a purple bruise spread downward from her right eye. The cuts had bled again, and Andy knelt to wipe away the grime that had soaked into her freckles.

"You did it," Andy said softly.

"Rebel did it." Barbara's smile lit up her face.

"He's a great horse." Andy hugged her. "But you're a winner, and you'll always be a winner, and tonight you and Rebel showed them all."

A crowd had gathered around them. Wilson pushed his way to the horse's side. Barbara's smile faded. For a moment she had felt so good. She would never feel that good again. Barbara took a deep breath, squared her shoulders, and did what she knew she had to do.

She handed the reins to Wilson and hugged Rebel for the last time. "He belongs to you," she said, her voice crisp, her gaze steady, choking back the tears that threatened to flood her eyes. She wouldn't cry. She wouldn't let anyone see her cry. But her small shoulders quivered as she stroked the big sorrel's neck.

The rancher grabbed the reins and turned to face Gabriel, anger embedded deeply in his face.

"You've caused me enough trouble, old man," he said, spitting out each word as though it were distasteful, "and it's gonna cost you plenty."

Gabriel scratched his chin.

Barbara stepped boldly forward. "I'm sorry I took him, Mr. Wilson," she apologized. "I didn't mean to. I didn't come out to your ranch to steal Rebel. I only wanted to see him again. When the fire started, I just got scared, and I ran." Her voice was strangely calm. Barbara tilted her chin meekly and added, "I only wanted to ride Rebel one last time. That's all. It was wrong. I shouldn't have done it. But I did, and I know Rebel belongs to you."

"You're bringing him back just a little late to do either one of us any good," Wilson answered, his face twisted in disdain. "I hope you know you were disqualified."

"Yes, sir."

"There was no way you could win."

"I know."

"Wilson," Gabriel interrupted, "it doesn't do anybody

219

any good to lock up the gate after the chickens have already flown the coop. Let's me an' you talk business a minute, man to man."

The rancher's eyes narrowed, and he looked askance at the old man. He didn't trust Gabriel. He didn't like to deal with Gabriel. The old man was shrewd, and he would cheat and lie if he had to, and nobody ever got the best of him in a trade.

"What's on your mind?" he asked warily.

"Well," Gabriel said, "Rebel ain't no good to you anymore. The season's over. Your daughter got what she wanted, and she didn't need Rebel to get it."

Wilson looked toward the arena, and he saw Sharon riding slowly and proudly toward him, holding the championship trophy that bore her name. Her head was thrown back and there was a smirk on her face. It didn't make any difference what people thought. It didn't make any difference what people said. She, Sharon Wilson, would always be the champion. She had the official, genuine golden trophy to prove it.

It gleamed in the moonlight. It matched her smile. Wilson's face softened.

"Sharon don't need Rebel anymore," Gabriel continued, "and Lord knows you've already got enough prized horseflesh runnin' around out there to stock just about every ranch between here and the Pecos River. I know. I birthed most of 'em and take care of the rest of 'em. They've all got fancy papers and bloodlines. Rebel ain't got nothin'. One more horse ain't gonna do nothin' but get in your way."

220

"So what are you suggesting?"

Gabriel pulled a tattered, dirt-stained envelope from his coat pocket and handed it to Wilson. "Here's the twenty-five hundred dollars you gave me for the horse. I ain't spent a dime of it. It's all there, just like you stacked it. You can have it. An' we'll take Rebel back home."

"You trying to buy the horse back?"

Gabriel scuffed a boot in the dirt. "I reckon I am."

Barbara looked up at her grandfather in amazement. She couldn't believe what she was hearing. She had dreamed that Rebel would forever run in her own back pasture, but she knew that dreams never came true, not in Caprock anyway.

"It's gonna cost you a little more to get him back," Wilson said flatly.

Gabriel nodded. "I thought it probably would."

"Five hundred more."

Gabriel sighed and turned away, disappointment cutting deep into his eyes. His shoulders slumped and his voice broke. It was barely audible. "I ain't got it," he said.

Wilson folded his arms and shifted his weight confidently. "Then you lose again," he said.

Barbara wilted.

The dream began to fade.

Luke suddenly stepped forward and pulled a handful of dirty, wrinkled bills from his hip pocket. "Gabe," he said, "here's the seventy-five dollars I owe you for taking care of my chickens during the blight."

"I ain't forgot how you nursed my prize bull back to health when he was dying," Harmon yelled from the back of the crowd. "You never sent me a bill, but you should have. It was worth more than a hundred and fifty, but that's all I got on me."

Juanita Madrone pressed twenty-five dollars into the old man's hand. "The colt wouldn't have made it if you hadn't been there," she said.

One by one, the small farmers and ranchers gathered around Gabriel and paid their outstanding debts. Fifty dollars came from Albert, who hadn't forgotten about the twin calves; twenty-five from Marcie McCready who had the sweetest melons in Caprock ever since the old man taught her to soak her seeds in sweet milk overnight before planting them; seventy-five from Roy Swanson who never bought a cow at anybody's auction until Gabriel gave his approval; and twenty-five from Garcia who no longer had a sick goat on his hands.

The old man slowly counted the money, then handed it to Wilson. "Here's four hundred," he said. "An' I believe you still owe me a hundred for de-horning those heifers of yours. So I guess that just about makes us even."

"Not quite."

A wolfish smile touched Wilson's lips.

In the past, Gabriel had beaten him in a deal or two. He would admit it. Some of the townspeople had even laughed at him behind his back.

They wouldn't laugh anymore.

This time, it was Gabriel B. Spencer who would be squirming.

"How about the land, Gabe?" Wilson asked. "I believe you also owe me back the deed for those six acres I gave you."

The old man nodded. He pulled the deed from his hip pocket and stared at it for a long time. For a week Barbara had owned the land free and clear, and there was nothing more valuable to him than good, honest dirt. He had spent his whole life trying to pay for it. He had lost the land once or twice, but always managed to get it back. For a week, it had been his granddaughter's, and now he was losing it again. Gabriel sighed and placed the deed in Wilson's hand.

"A man deserves what's rightfully his," Gabriel said, "and so does a little girl."

The rancher grinned. It was, he thought, a good day for the Wilsons, a red-letter day. Sharon had her championship trophy, and he had beaten Gabriel B. Spencer at his own game. What was more important, he had beaten the old horse trader in front of just about everybody who was somebody in Caprock.

He gloated. "Gabe," Wilson said, "I'm afraid you're gonna lose your reputation as a wheeler and dealer. The girl's getting the horse. You aren't. All you wound up with is a mortgage on six acres that you can't pay for."

Gabriel gazed out toward the prairie and fished a cheap cigar out of his coat pocket. He bit the end off and spit it out.

"I guess I'll pay it off at one hundred and thirty-eight dollars and forty cents a month," he answered. "At least, I'll pay it every month I can afford it."

Wilson pitched Rebel's reins to Barbara. "And Gabe," he said triumphantly, "you didn't get anything to boot this time."

For the first time, Gabriel smiled, and that old familiar twinkle returned to his eyes.

"That's where you're wrong, Warren," he said. "I did get something to boot." He reached down and took Barbara's small hand in his and squeezed it. "I got me a genuine, one-of-a-kind granddaughter."

Barbara leaned her head against his arm, and they walked out into the darkness together, leading Rebel back home where they all belonged. Wilson might have the land, but they had each other, and Gabriel knew he would never lose what was important to him again.